Death's Servant

FIRST PREQUEL NOVEL OF
THE V V INN SERIES
~ JON'S TALE ~

C.J. ELLISSON

Red Hot Publishing
P.O. BOX 651193, STERLING VA, 20165-1193

Copyright 2013 C.J. Ellisson
All Rights Reserved

Print ISBN 9781938601354

PUBLISHER'S NOTE
This is a work of fiction. Names, characters, places, and incidents are either the products of the author's imagination or are used fictitiously, and any resemblance to actual persons, living or dead ;-), business establishments, events, or locales is entirely coincidental.

This book is dedicated to my parents,
Margery and Jerry Stern.
Thank you for always believing I could do
anything I set my mind to

CHAPTER ONE

"Jon!" Romeo's deep voice follows as I stride quickly down the hall. "Get back here."

I round the top of the stairs and descend at full speed, skipping steps in my haste to leave. Anger pulses like a living beast beneath my skin. If I don't get the hell out of here, my alpha and I will come to blows.

The urge to *fight*, to answer the call of my inner wolf, colors my vision, tinting the werewolf pack's large home in a wash of red haze. Claws itch to descend through my clenched fists, and the brush of fur waiting to erupt tingles my skin.

"This is not over." Romeo's booming shout thunders through the house. "Get back here now, or don't ever come back!"

This time he's getting what he threatens. What's so crazy about suggesting a support network for wolves? Why am I suddenly the object of scorn and ridicule? Is organizing packs somehow a threatening concept to our way of life?

A tiny voice inside whispers, *Your suggestion of such a change goes against everything a werewolf pack stands for.*

Could that be true? Would instilling communication among hundreds of Weres hurt us as a species?

I block the denials I've heard for months. Doesn't make sense. Could Romeo's resistance stem from something bigger? Should I listen to the gossip saying I've evolved into an alpha faster than anyone expected? There is only one male alpha per pack, not two; one mated pair deciding the fate of their wolves, and those who don't agree must leave. Or fight for supremacy.

I barrel out the front door and sprint toward the detached garage, where a few of the single wolves have bedrooms in the space above the cars. I throw open the door, the heavy steel bouncing off the siding in my unchecked rage. I need to talk to Lori, my werewolf girlfriend in the pack. I'm ready to leave and want her with me.

My inner beast gnashes its teeth, ready for a challenge, eager to return and face the man who saved my life over a year ago. Tamping down the temptation, I rush the inner stairs three at a time. The scent of half a dozen wolves lies heavy in the confined space, confusing the rational part of my mind struggling to remain in control.

I recall the past in an effort to still my raging desires—I owe this man my life. Romeo found me lost and afraid when I awoke in the hospital, uncertain of what I'd become. Elsa, his wife, sensed immediately I was different, discouraging her mate to allow me into their pack. Romeo didn't care. He recognized me for what I truly was—a scared college kid who didn't know what the fuck happened to his well-ordered life.

When I reach the upper hall, I'm jolted out of my calming reverie by sounds of passion. I smile, wondering who Kotsana has lured to his waterbed now.

"That's it, baby," a familiar female voice coos softly. "You know I like it good and deep."

The instant anger near the surface of my mind threatens to overwhelm me. I stop cold—leaning a hand on the wall, gasping to catch my breath—while my packmate screws my girlfriend beyond his shut bedroom door. I close my eyes for a moment, trying to block images conjured by the sound of the big wolf making waves on his water mattress.

A soft panting noise reaches my ears and I know what's next—Lori's about to peak and scream to the high heavens. I wasn't sure if I loved her or if my feelings were caught up in the passion of our relationship. But all I feel right now is a white hot fury and a desire to tear someone apart with my bare hands, limb from limb.

Before I think through my actions, the doorknob to Kotsana's room is in my hand and I tear the door off the frame. The sound of splintering wood rips through the air and freezes them both on the bed. Lori's mouth opens in a silent *O* of shock.

I surge into the room and loom over their naked, sweating bodies. "Two-timing bitch!"

Lori grabs a sheet to cover herself as Kotsana looks at me with cool, calm eyes.

The Were hoists himself off her pliant body to lean

against the headboard. "Careful, Jon." His deep voice rumbles across the space between us as he raises his hands in a placating gesture. "She's not your mate and she wanted this."

I look at the silky dark hair framing Lori's elfin face. Her huge cornflower blue eyes shimmer with excitement. My heart hardens when she reaches a hand to fondle her own nipple.

"Want to join us, Jon?" Her other hand snakes to stroke Kotsana's still erect cock. "I bet the three of us could have some fun." Her head tilts to the side and she looks at her lover, perhaps trying to judge if he's game.

I knew she was a randy bitch, and she's certainly been pouring off sexual pheromones every waking hour of the day, but I honestly thought I satisfied her and we were building something.

Kotsana looks my way, recognizes my slow burn of barely controlled rage, and moves her hand from his body.

The second she's no longer touching him, I lunge across the bed, lugging her off the mattress by her arms. "You think it's funny to play more than one guy, don't you?" I grasp her shoulders and shake her hard, hoping her brain rattles in that pretty little head. "Just because you can fuck every unattached wolf you meet, doesn't mean you should."

I toss her unresisting form in the direction of the door and advance on Kotsana. "You knew she was with me."

His dark brown eyes flit to the floor, not meeting mine. "She smelled so damn good."

My hands curl over the bigger man's biceps and, in a move I'm sure I'll regret in a few minutes, I haul his naked ass from the bed and drag him toward the closed window. "Next time you bed a horny werewolf, make sure *she's* not sleeping with someone higher than *you* in your own freakin' pack." Kotsana's face changes to fear as he looks over his shoulder, working out what I plan to do. Panic pours off his larger frame, goading me to savagery at his show of weakness. "You'll have time to think about the wisdom of bed-hopping while you heal."

And with that, muscles bunch in my thighs and across my back as I throw the heavier man through the glass window. I turn back to Lori as she's scrambling into her discarded clothing. The tinkle of falling glass and a dull thud reach my ears, followed by screams of pain. The big man lies shrieking on the asphalt driveway below, and I couldn't care less.

"Jon, please." Fear etches the delicate lines of her face. "Let me explain."

I push by her, resisting the urge to pick her up and toss out her cheating ass with Kotsana. "What is left to explain? That the sex we had this morning wasn't enough for you? That the three orgasms I gave you while you screamed your love for me left you wanting?" I storm away, past two bedrooms, to the one we shared.

"Wait, Jon. Please!"

My fists clench at my side, anger boiling within me as I spin around to face her. "We're through! I'm done with this pack and the sex free-for-all you take as the status quo." Moisture gathers in my eyes, blurring my vision. "And to think, I came here hoping to take you with me. What a fucking joke."

Lori's face collapses and she starts to bawl. "Jon, no, don't go like this. We can work it out."

I slam my fist into the wall near her head, destroying the dry wall and the two-by-four behind it. "How can we possibly move beyond this when I still envision you reaching for his dick and inviting me to join?" I pull my hand from the hole, staring at the dry wall dust while ragged breaths steal past my lips. "Who the hell does that?" I whisper while looking into her clear blue eyes. "Who would twist what we had the way you did?"

She turns her face away, unable to meet my gaze any longer. Not having her with me is for the best. I can't imagine how in the hell I thought she was a good choice, in any sense of the word.

Lori hugs her arms around her curvy torso and sinks to the floor in the hall. I leave her to wallow in tears and quickly pack my bags, grabbing anything of personal value and all the clothes I can cram into the two large duffels.

The whole encounter, from tossing Kotsana out the window to making my way to the driveway, took less than five minutes. One of the other female Weres, Deneishia, crouches over the injured man on the asphalt.

Uncaring, I ignore his moans of pain and her calls for assistance. I stalk past them, climb inside my jeep, start it, and peel out of the Manitoba pack compound as fast as I can.

Romeo will get his wish.
I'll never come back—no matter what.

CHAPTER TWO

I drive for hours that stretch into days. No clear destination in mind besides crossing the Canadian border into the States. The idea of heading to my hometown in Williamsburg, Virginia occurs to me, but I dismiss it realizing the unanswerable questions I'd be faced with.

My folks think I died over a year ago in the hospital due to complications during the night I was attacked. Romeo and Elsa advised that my family was unsafe with me near them, and helped to feign my death.

Slowing to a stop for the red light ahead, a burn bubbles from my stomach at the thought of Romeo. Damn stubborn man. We're in the twenty first century, for Christ's sake. Who the hell wouldn't think organizing fellow supernaturals might be a smart idea? Oh, that's right, every damn alpha stuck in the nineteenth century.

My fingers tighten around the steering wheel, frustration and Were strength threatening to break the plastic. I loosen my grip when a horn honks behind me.

The traffic light is green and I'm not sure how long I've been sitting here ignoring it. Maybe it's time for a break. A glance at the dashboard clock reveals it's way past noon and I haven't eaten since the last refill for gas around dawn.

Awareness of my surroundings leaks back into perspective, diminishing the dull anger and some of the resentment I left in Canada. The clear May day shines on the green-shrouded highway, lush trees crowding the two-lane stretch. A road sign comes into view proclaiming I'm ten miles from Lovettsville.

Holy shit, I'm in northern Virginia. Huh. Guess I did unconsciously drive to where I'm most comfortable.

Lovettesville is several hours from my folks, so I'm unlikely to run into anyone here who knows me. Sounds like a good place to stop for a meal.

After a few minutes I angle my dust-covered jeep into a parking spot outside an old-fashioned diner. I cut the engine and ease open the truck door. Humidity hits me like a wet glove and the air seems heavier in my lungs. The sweet smell of new growth and distant tilled earth greet my sensitive nose. The warmth of the sun heats my skin while I stretch the miles from my aching muscles.

The parking lot contains eight cars, not bad for after two o'clock. Maybe the food here will be decent. Anything's better than the gas station food I've had for two days straight. Last night I stayed in a cheap motel after a cop told me I couldn't sleep in the cab of my jeep, even if he did agree it was silly law. The shower did me good and the change of clothes was well needed after days of hard driving.

A quaint bell jangles above the glass door at my entrance. Vacant stools line the counter, but I make my way to a booth. Hours of concentrated focus on the road have left me jittery and wired, yet physically weary and exhausted. I'm not used to feeling anything other than extreme mellowness within the pack.

Maybe coming back to Virginia was not a good idea. Being here feels familiar and yet awkward all at once.

A plastic coated menu slides across the table into view, pulling me out of the déjà vu moment. A throat clears nearby and draws my gaze up the pink dress of the waitress who brought the menu.

A slim woman, with a becoming smile, a blush to her cheeks, and a cap of shiny dark hair waits patiently with an order pad at the ready. "What can I get for you, hon?" She smiles again, revealing a dimple near one corner of her upturned mouth.

I smile in response, the reaction automatic. "Coffee first, please. Black." She dips her chin in acknowledgment. I gesture toward the menu. "Do you have any recommendations?"

"For today's lunch special we've got marinated chicken—grilled and served over fresh greens." She smiles again. "But anything you get will be good. The cook does a great job."

I nod, careful to squash the frown I instinctively feel forming at the thought of ordering only a salad, and open the menu to see what else they offer.

"I'll get your coffee and come back for your order." She bustles away, trailing a faint whiff of werewolf pheromones in her wake. I sit up straighter and turn in the booth, following her retreat behind the counter.

Holy crap. She's like me. What are the chances my first real meal since Canada is served by a werewolf? Was I pulled here subconsciously? Like pheromones in the air or something?

Or fate. Maybe this is where you were meant to be.

I tense, worried I'll be discovered by my scent and that I might be infringing on another pack's territory. I've got to get her alone to question her.

Yeah, like that's going to be easy. What young waitress wouldn't welcome a private talk with a stranger?

A casual examination of the restaurant reveals it isn't as full as the parking lot would indicate. The closest diner to me sits three booths down.

Maybe I could ask about the local pack situation out here in the open? Or should I push my own scent into the air and see if she responds?

She's returning with my coffee and I make a split decision. I reach inside and mentally call up an image of my old pack. Cool dark woods zip by as I race in my wolf form, surrounded by the well-known bodies that my inner beast naturally trusts.

She sets the coffee on the table, and stares. Her nostrils flare and pupils dilate. "Well, what do we have here?" Interest leaps into her eyes. "You don't look familiar. New in town?"

I nod, reaching for my cup of coffee. The warmth from the ceramic seeps into my grasp, spreading up my hands. "Just stopping for a meal." I keep my tone neutral, hoping to not alarm her. "Not poaching land."

Sadness sweeps across her face, quickly replaced by good humor. "You don't need to worry about that. There's no claim here."

My eyebrows jump up my forehead. "Really?" She nods and a stillness steals over me. How could she be a lone wolf on her own? Or are there others but no alpha?

Innate instinct creeps up, startling me with the depth of desire coiling in my gut. The need to rule and dominate other wolves washes through me, surprising me with its ferocity. *She will bow to my wolf.*

Where the hell did that come from? I'm not eager to lead a pack, nor do I know enough to keep one safe.

After a slight hesitation, a warm invitation crosses her face. "Sure you don't want to stay in town a while? Get to know the area? There's lots of open ground to run."

A feeling of *home,* so long suppressed under Romeo's lead, warms my heart. "Maybe I will." Impulsively, I extend a hand in greeting. "Hi, I'm Jon."

That adorable blush I noticed earlier comes back, spreading up her neck as she reaches for my hand. Hers eyes dart toward the floor before briefly returning to me and flitting away. "Raine."

Oh, she's familiar with a pack, all right. That was definitely a submissive wolf reaction. "Pretty name for an even prettier lady."

She smiles, a flirtatious look lighting her eyes. "Thanks. Now, what can I get you to eat?"

My stomach grumbles right on cue. I laugh, the

stress from Manitoba rolling off my shoulders like it never existed. "I'll start with two steaks. Medium rare, please."

She winks and nods, sashaying her hips as she walks away to place my order.

About fifteen minutes later, Raine returns with my meal. I clear my throat as the full platter slides across the table. "You wouldn't know of any place hiring, would you?"

"Are you okay with manual labor?" Her dark blue eyes linger on my torso as I nod. "There's a huge construction boom in the county. Good money. If you don't own tools you could hire on to an existing crew or find landscaping work pretty easy."

I studied botany at James Madison University, the campus farther south, where the werewolf attack changed my life forever. My dream at school was to someday own a nursery and landscaping company. Hope for a new life blossoms in me for the first time since leaving Canada. Maybe it *was* fate that brought me back to Virginia. "Does the diner keep a recent newspaper behind the counter?"

CHAPTER THREE

I start work immediately with a local landscaper and am quickly promoted to leading a crew—my knowledge of plants and ability to speak Spanish the driving forces behind the advancement. Today is Friday and I plan to ask out the cute waitress for dinner. I had breakfast at the diner this morning, when she first arrived at work, so I know she's got the evening shift off.

The bell over the door jingles when I enter, sending my nerves into overdrive. A warm smile lights Raine's face when she sees me.

"Nice to see you again, Jon." She glances at her watch. "My shift is almost over." A faint flash of disappoint flashes over her features. "Damn. Looks like someone else will serve you."

"I was hoping you might join me for dinner." I clear my throat, nervous for the first time in months. "You know—someplace else—not here. Like a date."

Raine glances down my body, noting my freshly changed clothes. "I'd like that, Jon." The gleam in her eye turns predatory, triggering an answering heat low in my middle. "I've only got a casual sundress with me, is that okay?"

"You could be dressed in rags and I'd still be happy to take you out."

"Aren't you sweet." She smiles, the humor only halfway reaching her eyes. "Give me ten minutes."

The young Were retreats to the back hall where the employee lockers stand near the manager's office. There was a lurking sadness in her eyes when she agreed to dinner. I hope over our meal I can coax out of her whatever brought it on. My wolf wants to make her *mine,* and the human part of me doesn't quite know what to do with the new urges.

The noise of the Blue Ridge Grill fades into the background as I watch Raine polish off her second burger. "For a tiny little thing, you sure can keep up." My face freezes in horror as I realize I just told the attractive woman I brought to dinner that she eats a lot.

Raine's laughter trips from her lips in the first show of genuine humor I've seen from her all night. "Oh my God—you should see your face right now, Jon. Classic!" She wipes the tears from her eyes with the end of her napkin. "No one would accuse you of being a silver-tongued devil, that's for sure." She smiles to show she's teasing then shrugs a slim shoulder under her pale blue sundress. "What can I say? I work so much it's hard to keep the pounds on." Her face sobers, the humor draining as fast as it came, and she looks away. "We do have an excellent metabolism."

Something doesn't add up. Waitressing might be hard work and a lot of hours on your feet, but a healthy werewolf who eats like she just did shouldn't be waif-like thin. Maybe she has a second job. Trying to make ends meet on tips can't be easy. Especially without a pack for support or a werewolf roomie to share the rent.

I want to ask how she's doing financially, curious if she does indeed have a second job and why, but something holds me back. We don't know each other well enough for me to start prying, and asking might scare her off. If I want to start over here in Virginia, I'll need to slowly bring wolves to me, and that won't happen if I come on too strong.

Slowly bring wolves to me? Where the hell are these thoughts coming from? That sounds a lot like alpha tendencies rearing an ugly head. Am I ready for my own pack? After Manitoba, I sure as hell don't want to *join* another one. Could I become a true alpha and protect others of my kind?

The memories of Romeo—breaking up fights, mentoring others unhappy with their dual nature, and financially supporting ones who needed it—flare bright across my mind. We may have clashed, but he took good care of his wolves.

No, I'm not ready for another pack, even one of my own. Maybe that will change in the coming months, who knows.

After a moment, Raine's tinge of sadness disappears and a slow seductive smile crosses her face. The sexual pheromones I've suppressed all week seep out little by little. There's no denying that even sad, she's delectable to my raging libido. Raine's bare foot rubs my calf toward my knee. Instantly, the room narrows to the beguiling young woman and her seductive smile. Her arousal taints the air, calling me to act.

I reach across the distance between us and pull her slim fingers to my lips. "I could just eat you up."

Her brows rise. "Really, now?" A saucy superiority burns from her eyes. "You sound suspiciously like the Big Bad Wolf hitting on Red Riding Hood."

A sharp bark of laughter erupts from me, breaking the tension. I really suck at flirting. "Can't blame a guy for trying." Resigned to the fact we may not have any fun tonight if based on my flirting skills, and her wandering foot could be her way of teasing, I rise from the table and offer my hand. "Want to go out for a night cap or should you take me back to my jeep at the diner?"

"I know of a nice bar in downtown Leesburg." She winks and takes my hand. "It's not far."

Hope stirs in my heart as we exit the restaurant. Maybe things are picking up.

An hour later in a dimly lit bar, there's no way I'm mistaking Raine's intentions. She's been stroking my growing erection through my jeans for the last ten minutes. Randy bitch—and I say that with the utmost respect for the fascinating werewolf—just nibbled on my ear and told me to kiss her.

I stare into her midnight blue depths and whisper, "Not here." I brush my lips faintly over hers, promising more to come in private. I've never been one for public displays of affection and I don't want our first kiss to be surrounded by strangers.

She nods and stands, adjusting her dress as she rises. The shift of fabric releases her aroused scent into the air. A hard fist of want punches me in the gut, requiring me to use all the restraint I possess to not dart out the doors toward the parking lot, dragging the tempting woman with me.

The steady sexual partners available in a large wolf pack are both a curse and a blessing. On one hand, having an increased libido and a host of willing single partners is great. On the other, trying to establish any kind of true intimacy or a real relationship is next to impossible.

Maybe that's why many Weres find their life mates outside their pack. Summer hunting expeditions, the rare regional pack gatherings I've heard tales of, or dating humans seem to be the best way to find a lifelong mate. No one ever mentioned the idea of two loners, like me and Raine, hooking up—but it certainly seems possible now that I'm living it.

The late May night wraps its moist hold around us as we exit the bar and make our way to Riane's car. Short pants of breath reach my ears in the dark, indicating she's as turned on as I am at the prospect of being together. Her warm hand links with mine as hot coils of anticipation writhe in my gut.

Raine tugs our clasped hands, changing our

direction from her car door to the nose of her vehicle, where the shadows from the building lie deep. She presses my back against the wood siding, leaning in to kiss me. Our raging desires, carefully held in check inside the bar, explode. Her hot mouth latches onto mine as her soft body molds to my front.

Eager hands reach under my t-shirt, lingering over my abs on their path upward. Raine breaks our kiss, whispering in a husky voice, "My, my, my, Jon." Her nimble fingers find my hardened nipples and she tweaks them with a twist. "You're hiding quite a nice body under here."

Heat races over me, along with a flash of Lori touching me like this a mere two weeks ago. I clasp her hands, settling mine firmly over hers to help block the unwanted memories. "What do you expect from a man who works outside for a living? A soft body and pasty complexion?"

The sexy Were nips my bottom lip lightly. "I guess I wasn't expecting you to be so... hard." Her hand slips free of my hold and skims down to cup my erection through my pants.

A soft growl erupts from me as I pivot, reversing our position and pinning her supple body to the wall. "You like to move fast, don't you, Raine?" I press forward with my hips, rubbing my arousal against her middle, effectively pushing her hand away as well.

I bow to gently bite the tender flesh between her ear and shoulder. "All 'pretty in pink' in that waitress outfit..." Another nip to her heated flesh draws a gasp from the young woman. "I never would've expected the fire..."

She reaches two hands to grab my hair, pulling me up to her mouth. "Well then, Jon, looks like you underestimated me." Raine plasters her mouth to mine, ratcheting up my already raised hormones. Lust courses through me, pushing to barrel ahead, to take her—wherever she wants me—even if it's in a parking lot.

In a few moments our kiss breaks, leaving us both panting and grasping at the other's body, desperate to rein our passion despite the waves of desire crashing over us. "Want to come back to my place?" she asks. There's a desperate edge to her voice that gives me pause. "It's out past Purcellville."

It would be so easy to take her offer. To follow her the distance to wherever she lives and make love to her all night. But things went fast with Lori, too. And look where that got me—dangling on the end of her raw sex appeal and oblivious to her baser nature of a two-timing horny Were.

I take a small step back and reach up to cup Raine's cheeks in my hands. "Would you hate me if I said 'no'?" Confusion mixes with the lust in her eyes. "I like you, Raine." I kiss her again. "I want to go slow."

Her spine straightens. "Uh... what?" She makes a last grab for my pants. "You want me. Why deny it?" She wraps a hot hand over me and begins to stroke. "We can make all the noise we want and no one will hear us." A cold, evaluating look comes into her eyes, making me wonder why she's so desperate for my attention.

I kiss her once more, ignoring the warning bells that she could be another manipulating she-wolf out to break my heart, and pour my pent up sexual frustration into the kiss before I break away. "I definitely want you." My breath pants in the darkness as I seek her eyes in the dim light. "You know that, right? You deserve more than a night of lust on our first date—*we* deserve more." Her calculating look fades, to be replaced by one of disbelief. "I want to make a life here, and I'd like to see if that can be a life that has you in it for longer than just a few hours of sex."

Raine slumps against the wall, her aggression and passion draining out of her at my words. "Wow, you really know how to take the wind out of a girl's sail—but, in a classy sort of way." She runs a hand through her short hair, pushing it back from her face. A small smile lights her features in the night. "At least I know you want me and it could lead to more."

"What do you say?" I can't believe I'm talking this woman out of jumping my bones, but until I get to know her better, it's for the best. "Want to go on a second date?"

Her face closes and she looks into the distance. "Sure. I might be up for a going out again."

CHAPTER FOUR

Next week I ask her out again. "How about it, Riane? Ready for date number two?" I wiggle my eyebrows suggestively, hoping to make her smile.

She's been distant the past few days when I visited the diner to eat. Something has changed on her end, and I'm not sure what.

Her eyes dart away before she answers. "Sorry, Jon, I'm busy tonight."

My stomach plummets. "How about tomorrow?"

A sadness creeps into her gaze as she shakes her head. "I'm busy all weekend. Sorry."

I nod as she leaves to wait on a customer, taking her refusal like an adult, but curious to find out what happened. She was climbing all over me last Friday. It makes no sense.

I've eaten at the diner every day, even if Raine wasn't working. Some days we don't get to do more than exchange a few pleasantries, but it's worth it. Being in her presence soothes me. I've never been away from other wolves for this long and hadn't realized how much I needed her companionship.

Last week our flirting was intense. But I was still too raw from Lori's betrayal to want to leap into anything—did I screw things up by waiting too long to ask her out again? Getting to know her through casual conversation felt refreshing, something I lacked with every other wolf I'd been with prior.

I wasn't ready to follow through on the lust we explored on our first date. But now I am. I've rented a small apartment and acquired some decent furnishings. I have the beginnings of my own den to share. We may not turn into anything permanent, but I aim to find out.

There's something about the young woman that calls to me. Resigned to the fact she said no for tonight, I grab a free spot at the counter and settle in for dinner. Determined to not act like a jerk, I wave to the young Were when she glances my way. Her shoulders relax and her face softens. She's pinned her short dark hair behind her ears with butterfly barrettes, the style making her look even younger than her twenty-one years.

Unlike the robust health and curves of Lori, and most of the other female Weres in Manitoba, Raine has a delicacy to her. I'm not normally attracted to overly slender women, but she pulls my protective alpha nature to the surface. I want to coddle and cosset her, protect her from harm and wrap myself around her while she sleeps.

Every time she walks past me, my wolf leaps to the

surface, eager to rub against her for companionship. I like this casual state of arousal I'm in when around her. My senses feel heightened and the world looks fresher. Is it being free from the burden of the Manitoba pack or the stirrings of what will be a brighter future here in Virginia?

My meal arrives and the smell of homemade cobbler drifting from the kitchen reminds me of home with my folks. Could I approach them now that I'm stronger and no longer a risk to their safety? Was Romeo's suggestion of severing all contact with family truly the only option available? I tamp down the slow burn of anger coiling in my gut. No purpose in dwelling on the past.

Raine's eyes lock with mine across the length of the counter. She's pouring coffee for a patron, allowing her attention to wander my way. I deliberately focus on lustful thoughts, encouraging my sexual pheromones to blanket the air. Raine becomes distracted by the scent, and over pours, spilling coffee to the saucer below the cup.

Her face flushes while she reaches for extra napkins, her eyes flick my way, a desperate edge in their depths. She finishes cleaning and scurries to the back room, avoiding me. Interesting reaction. I wonder what has her so jumpy. Female Weres don't normally react to an alpha's heat by running away. Within a few heartbeats everyone near me is smiling, their sexual energies higher than normal. I tone down the pressure; worried I may have overplayed my hand.

She's a tough nut to crack.

Are you going to let a scrumptious werewolf ripe for the picking slip from your grasp so easily?

Damn. I'm used to female werewolves chasing *me*. This hard-to-get crap is a whole new experience, especially after her blatant invitation in the parking lot.

You could have bruised her ego when you turned her down.

But then why the flirting since then?

Are you an alpha or a puppy? Show her what you want.

Decision made, I toss my napkin on my plate and make my way to the back hallway. The tingling awareness of hunting prey stretches across my skin, enticing my wolf to draw closer to the surface. This is fun.

Wait a minute—there's a back door at the end of the corridor I was unaware of. Hmm... I wonder if she was planning to slip out unseen to avoid me. Definitely time to find out what the hell is going on.

The ladies room door opens three feet away and Raine emerges. She's changed into a snug pair of hip-hugging jeans and a tight t-shirt. A strip of honey colored skin is exposed between the two, the flat planes of her stomach teasing me to touch. A small squeak escapes her when she sees me.

I push out sexual lust when I whisper her name. "Hi, Raine." She shudders at the sound. "You weren't going to ditch me without saying goodnight, were you?"

She stumbles away to press against the rear door. "Uh... no. I have to be somewhere." Her breath huffs out, her gaze sliding away from me, to her escape.

I nod, shifting position against the wall, bringing her attention back to me without having to step any closer. "You seem to be avoiding me lately. Then the refusal for another date. What's going on?"

The scent of her arousal drifts in the air toward me, proving she's not as unaffected by me as she'd like me to believe. "Can you tone down the sexual vibe?" Her voice cracks with the strain. "I'm barely hanging by a thread here."

Immediately I cut off the outpouring of pheromones. The air clears in the space of a few heartbeats. "Done. Now, come clean. I know you're interested and yet you've refused me for a second date. Did you lie about having a boyfriend?"

A shadow crosses her face. "No, I don't have a boyfriend, that was true. I just changed my mind about going out with you again so soon."

Her puckered nipples strain against the tight fabric of her shirt. Her breasts are small enough that she doesn't need a bra. Not wearing one works to my advantage—she can't hide her response to me.

A slow smile spreads across my mouth. I glance down at her chest and back up, purposely calling attention to her arousal. "Really? Your body begs to differ."

Heat suffuses her cheeks. She shrugs and her tone comes out flat. "We can't always get what we want."

I push off the wall and cross the hall to stand in front of her. "What happened, Raine? Last week you invited me back to your place."

Her eyes flick to the door again, her discomfort at

my nearness quite clear. "And you refused!" One tiny hand lifts to my chest, halting my advance when I would have pressed against her. "It turned out to be for the best." Her face shuts down. "I need to go."

The metallic click of the releasing door lock shatters the silence, spurring me into action at the sight of her disappearing form. I'm not giving up without a fight. I feel something for her dammit, even if I'm not sure what it is.

"Raine, wait!" I rush after her, catching the door before it closes, and leap down the three stairs to the back parking lot.

She turns, keys clutched in her hand, ready to get in her car. The anguish on her face fuels me forward. I close the space and pull her stiff form into my arms. Before I have a chance to think things through, I lower my lips to hers and capture her mouth in a kiss.

Ignoring the desire to plunder her softness, I hold back my animal instincts, tasting her sweetness in a tender brush of skin on skin. A spark of yearning burns between us and I deepen my pressure, gently running my tongue along her lower lip. With a soft moan she succumbs, opening her mouth to mine as stress melts from her body.

Running a hand over her silky cap of hair, I lightly cup her skull, angling her head for better access. Eager for more, my tongue ventures inside, licking her top teeth and sparring with her own shy advances.

Very soon our ragged breathing is the only sound in the deserted lot. I playfully nip her bottom lip and an anguished cry rips from her throat, right before she pushes me away.

"I like you, Jon. A lot." She raises a stiff arm to hold me at a distance. "But there are things going on that you're unaware of."

The passion boiling through my veins makes my voice harsher than I'd like. "What the hell is that supposed to mean?"

She jolts, like I've physically smacked her. Fear skitters across her face, chased away by firm resolve. "You need to leave northern Virginia." She yanks open her car door and rushes inside. The engine turns over while I stand with my mouth agape. "Trust me. It's for your own good."

CHAPTER FIVE

I sit in my jeep for thirty minutes, contemplating what the hell just happened. I know I didn't misread her attraction; our scorching hot kisses prove there's chemistry on both sides. Could she have some crazy ex-boyfriend stalking her and she lied to spare me the drama of having to face the nutjob?

A snort huffs through my nose. Highly unlikely a werewolf would worry about that kind of crap.

Or could she currently be involved with someone and she lied about being available? That idea rings more true than the first. But why sound so doom and gloom and cryptic, telling me it was better if I left for my own good? I shake my head, reining in the angry impulse to punch the steering wheel.

She said I didn't have to worry about poaching on existing pack territory, but how is it possible she's living as a lone wolf in an area I *know* is inhabited with other werewolves. I was attacked on campus by a werewolf only a few hours from here. Romeo and Elsa had been traveling on business when they heard of my bizarre animal attack.

The couple's outrageous explanation of my wounds sunk in only after I witnessed my own body healing at an unreal speed. They assured me the attacking wolf had been dealt with by the local pack. Could Loudoun County, just a little ways north in the same state, have lone wolves and no ruling pack? Doesn't seem likely. And yet I was all too ready to swallow that line when Raine fed it to me. I grip the wheel in frustration, wishing I could rip it out and toss it through the darkening parking lot.

I want to call Romeo and ask advice, but can't risk it. There's no way he's ready to talk to me after the scene I made when leaving. I should be grateful he hasn't sent pack members out to haul my ass back to the fold. Maybe it's the whole alpha thing. He could be relieved I left because now we wouldn't have any physical confrontation.

Dammit! I punch the dash, my rage getting the best of me. If I hadn't stood frozen in shock I could have followed Raine and questioned her further. I'll have to wait until she's working again to corner her.

I'm not a quitter. I'll be damned if I walk away from her without a real reason.

That look on her face when I asked what was going on haunts me. Her slight recoil and the subsequent fear mean something. Resigned to the fact I won't get any answers tonight, I head home, determined to discover the truth.

Raine hasn't been at work for two days. Since I know which car is hers, I cruise by several times a day looking for it. At first I worried maybe she had someone drop her off, or borrowed someone else's car, just to avoid me. A casual stroll from me past the large windows to check out the wait staff working each shift confirmed she wasn't there. I even searched for her scent on the back stairs. Nothing.

When I finally see her battered Honda late on Sunday relief sweeps through me. Should I approach her inside at work, wait out here for the end of her shift, or just follow her home? My attempt to talk to her in the parking lot a few days ago didn't go well and I'm acutely aware the second option of following her home skirts perilously close to stalker behavior. Well, my actions of driving by several times a day were stalkerish, too, and that didn't stop me.

Before I decide on a suitable plan, the back door swings open and Raine walks down the steps. Her shoulders hunch forward and her thin arms wrap around her middle like she's cold despite the high temperatures hitting on the first day of June. She's not dressed for work and heads directly to her car, not sparing a glance around the lot in her haste.

Looks like my only option is the scary stalker following her home.

My jeep idles on the side of the road with the windows up. With any luck she won't smell I'm here and I'll be able to follow her. I slide down in the seat when she turns onto the road, waiting a few seconds before straightening and following. I ease off the shoulder and tail her car at a discrete distance. She continues on 15 South toward Purcellville. After a dozen or so miles, Raine takes the exit for town. I follow a hundred yards behind, glad it's not full dark yet when headlights could give away my position.

She takes a lot of turns, leading me deeper into undeveloped farmland and away from the construction sites mushrooming all over Loudoun County. She turns onto a long gravel drive. Thick trees and deep underbrush hide any glimpse of a house, and her bumper disappears beyond a bend as I pass the mouth of the driveway. Unwilling to risk discovery, I pull over a quarter of a mile past the entrance and shut off the jeep.

No other homes are close by. I roll down the window to sample the air. Scents of fertile dirt, new plant growth, and fresh horse manure stream in. Man, we are isolated—about three turns back we crossed into what I call *the boonies*. This is what I've heard the locals affectionately refer to as "horse country." Living most of my life in southern Virginia, I'm no stranger to desolate farmland, but to find it close to an area with one of the biggest construction booms in the state feels surreal.

The wind shifts and the pungent odor of wolves drifts over the lowered glass. My gut tightens in response. *Lone wolf*, my ass. There's a pack in this area and I've just stumbled onto their den. Why in the hell did she lie to me?

I quietly exit the jeep, keenly aware that walking uninvited onto their property could be the stupidest thing I've done in my life to date.

Is this the place she invited me to last week? Her being part of a pack changes the meaning of why she acted the way she did.

She's hiding something.

And as I slip into the dense greenery next to the driveway, my heart hardens with resolve—I intend to find out exactly what she's concealing.

Recent rain has left the ground spongy, making my every step absorbed by plump soil and new plants. The sun set while I trailed Raine to this isolated location, and the long twilight of late spring creates deep shadows between the thin trunks and undergrowth.

In a third of a mile or so, glimpses of red brick and a metal roof wink through the dense vegetation. Within a few minutes a huge structure and several smaller outbuildings come into view. Three stories high with a gabled roof and arched windows, the main house resembles a McMansion on steroids.

The new homes where I've been working don't even compare, and I thought those houses were huge. Either her pack is doing much better than Romeo's in Manitoba or this isn't their home.

The breeze shifts and the strong stink of werewolf lifts to reveal a fainter scent underneath. Blood cools in my veins as I realize I've encountered the odor before. It's the unmistakable stench of vampire.

Is this a vampire house and the wolves live here as well?

I tamp down my confusion and skirt the edge of the woods, slowly making my way onto the neatly trimmed grass, angling toward a far corner of the house.

A large detached garage comes into view with an array of expensive cars parked on the gravel. I see hood and grill ornaments for Mercedes, Lexus, and Porsche. Either they've got company or Raine's pack drives luxury cars. Her tiny battered Honda sits off near an even larger, one-story outbuilding farthest away.

I ease behind the garage, casually drifting from one darkened location to the next. Despite the obvious signs of habitation, no one walks the grounds nor do I see any movement through the windows. Huh. Wonder where everyone is?

I approach Raine's car, her familiar scent filling my nostrils. A quick glance reveals the car lies empty without even a candy wrapper to clutter its neatness. The area near her car door holds the strongest trace of her, the trail leading toward the large house, not one of the other outlying cottages or sheds.

I tense, unsure if the course I've taken in coming here is the wisest choice. I'm all alone and have no idea what I'll be facing. I shrug off my discomfort and follow Raine's last steps. I've come this far, might as well see it through to the end.

Like I suspected, she went to the backdoor of the main house. Sounds of local wildlife from the dense woods surrounding the house are strangely absent, as if they sensed my predator presence and refrained from further display. Before I decide to try the knob or knock, a groan meets my ears. The sound issues from the right, around the corner of the imposing brick façade.

I press my back to the sun-warmed surface and slink quietly along the outside wall, easing toward the noise. A large bay window protrudes, its panes free of fabric, allowing inhabitants a clear view of the peaceful woods beyond. The design style also offers me an unhindered view inside.

Two men in tuxedos stand with their backs to me, their attention focused on the dining room table before them. One brown-haired man stands taller than the other one with black hair. The shorter man leans forward, eagerness apparent in his body language. I follow his gaze and barely stifle my surprise in time.

Raine sits on the polished mahogany surface, knees spread to bracket her thighs outside the hips of a third tuxedo-clad man standing in front of her, leaning over her neck. Her head is tipped back, leaving her delicate throat exposed to the man's attentions.

His dark blond head angles across her throat. He appears to be kissing the skin there.

She groans again and the sound cuts through my heart like a knife. All this time I thought she wanted me, desired me as a possible mate. What an idiot I've been.

The man roughly pulls down the neck of her t-shirt to expose her breast. He grabs her flesh, squeezing hard. Raine gasps and thrashes her head to the side, allowing me to see her eyes are scrunched tightly closed, a look of discomfort showing in her features.

I jerk in surprise when one of the men, the taller one with brown hair, near the partly opened window speaks. "Go easy on her, Nathaniel." His voice holds strength and the man kissing Raine's neck loosens his hold on her small breast. "She donated last Wednesday and I'll not have you draining her more than necessary. She's a favorite of Dominic's and he's scheduled her for Friday."

A faint whiff of blood billows from under the wooden pane and fear grips my gut. As if confirming my horrified thoughts, a thin trail of red seeps down the young woman's skin, collecting in the hollow of her throat.

Dear God. They're vampires feeding off Raine.

By the casual sound of the tall man's comments, it must be a normal occurrence. Panic clogs my throat as I stand frozen in place, unable to turn away from the horrible display and afraid to move and be discovered.

Nathaniel ignores the vampire by the window, instead pressing a palm roughly between Raines legs, groping her through her jeans. She bucks at the added stimulation, a look of disgust crossing her face at her body's betrayal.

The second man standing near the window chuckles. "You're losing your touch, old man. She doesn't look like she's enjoying it."

Nathaniel raises his bloody mouth, feral eyes focusing on the man who spoke. Without a glance back at Raine, he slips his hand into her pants for a more intimate caress. "Want to wager who can get her off faster?"

Raine's eyes fly open and she looks toward the window, her eyes seeking out the tall brown-haired man who warned off Nathanial. She shakes her head side to side, fighting what the man's ministrations are making her feel.

A low growl starts deep in my throat. The alpha instinct to protect rages to the surface at her look of utter dejection and humiliation.

In a lightning fast move, the two men by the window spin around. The tall one leaps through the glass, tackling me.

Strong hands pin me to the ground as a rabid face full of dripping fangs leans toward me.

"And who do we have here?" The vampire sniffs the air near my neck. "You're the werewolf Raine was with earlier. The one she *said* left town no matter how she tempted him to stay."

I push up with my hips, trying to buck off the creature. We thrash until he grasps both my hands in his, pinning them above my head as if I were a weak child. The look on his maddened face sends additional adrenaline streaming through my body, pushing my inner wolf into a fight response.

The change boils under my skin, the wolf struggling to break my hold and meet this new threat. A growl of fury erupts from my throat as I brace to rip off his face with my teeth. The change begins and my jaw elongates into a muzzle full of sharp teeth. I lash out, snapping at the grinning vampire.

He avoids my attack and punches me in the face, harder than I've ever felt from an enraged Were. It momentarily halts my change, stunning me with the pain. He laughs and hits me again, effectively ending my retaliation.

"Come and join me, Thomas," my captor calls over his shoulder. "This one's fresh—and on the house."

The second vampire jumps through the window to crouch next to my side. Raine's scream of "no!" is the last thing to penetrate my consciousness as two sets of fangs descend upon me.

CHAPTER SIX

Pain radiates through my skull as my surroundings slowly come into focus. I'm lying on a cold, gritty floor. Weakness drags at my limbs, making it hard to raise my head. What the hell happened?

In a flash, the memory of intense pain and fear spiral through me, drawing a hard shudder in response.

A rustle nearby draws my attention to a blurry figure a few feet away. "Thank God," Raine's concerned voice reaches me. "You're finally awake." She sounds strained and nervous. Considering she's living with a group of blood sucking parasites—ones that will apparently jump on anything on their property and suck it almost dry—I can sympathize.

A cup is pressed to my lips, while a gentle hand slips behind my head to support me. "Here. Drink this."

Warm water flavored with something lemony trickles past my cracked lips. "If we get fluids in you it should speed up your healing." Despair clouds her pretty gaze. "Why? Why did you follow me, you stupid bastard?"

I sputter, but continue to drink. She takes the empty mug away and refills it from a nearby pitcher. I struggle to a seated position, finding my actions slowed by chains binding my limbs loosely to the wall behind me.

My vision clears as I glance around the room. Dim light from the naked overhead bulb does nothing to enhance the starkly empty space. Or should I call it a *cell*? The cinderblock walls and steel door emphasize my assumption.

What the fuck is going on here?

My coordination slowly returns and I reach for the full mug she's offering. I gulp half the contents before bothering to respond her question. "You really think my following you is the biggest issue to discuss, right now? What is this place?"

Raine settles on the floor next to me, resting the carafe on one splayed thigh. "I used to call it Hell." She smirks and meets my eye. "But after meeting you, and dreaming about freedom, I realize this place is worse."

I drain the cup and reach for the pitcher. "Worse than Hell?" I pour the tangy water, eager for more as my strength returns. "Sitting chained to a wall after being drained by two vampires... well, it's not Hell but it's not great, either."

Tears trickle down the young woman's face. "What would you call it after five years? What would you call it when you watch your friends die? What would you call it when you're forced to lure more of your kind here?"

"That depends. What exactly is 'here'?"

Raine looks toward the partially open door, her

gaze distant and sad. "It's a pretty prison. Not this room, obviously, but the big house. A prison decorated with lavish parties and forced entertaining."

I drink my lemon water, which is strangely making me feel a lot better than one would expect, and watch a shiver run over her. "This blood brothel is run by Cecil Davies. He's a vampire addicted to Were blood."

"Addicted to Were blood? A blood brothel? I didn't know the first was possible or the second even existed."

She looks at me and shakes her head in remorse. "Apparently the addiction is more common than I would've have guessed. Cecil has my whole pack bound to him as vampire servants. We can't refuse his commands—even ones that go against every fiber of our being."

Her overly flirtatious behavior when I first pulled into town makes more sense. She was *ordered* to bring more werewolves to feed this vampire's addiction. Maybe ordered to flirt with me as well.

"I don't understand. How many of you are here? How much blood can one vampire drink?"

"I don't know how much they can drink at once, but several feedings too close together have killed quite a few of us. Our pack was small to begin with, only twenty. Half of them died in the last eighteen months." She trails off and hangs her head, staring at the floor. "But I've brought in nine more over the years—three of which also died. And I'm not the only wolf bringing in victims."

A chill creeps down my spine. She meant to lead me here, just like the others. But she also warned me, telling me to leave town. Something doesn't add up. How did she resist her orders to bring me in?

"How did you lie to him about me?"

"I'm not sure. There is the obvious compulsion to obey burned into my brain, but apparently I could lie just enough regarding you to make him believe me." She looks at me with longing. "I wondered if it might mean we were destined to be... more to each other... if the situation was different."

My mind whirls, desperate to figure out a plan to save these wolves and myself. What is Cecil's security like? I recall two who attacked me as a third stood close by, feeding on Raine. "How many vampires live here?"

"Just him. The others come and pay to feast on werewolf blood... among other things. They use us like rag dolls, knowing we can heal from any damage they dole out."

Sickness coils in my stomach at the thought of all these people held against their will and made to service any vampire with enough money.

"How did all this happen? Where is your alpha? What happened to him and his mate?"

A sad look crosses her face as she fills my mug once more. "He was the third one taken. After that we all dropped like flies, bound to his call as our leader."

"Third? That means he knew what was going on...and..." The bastard led them into this Hell.

"Yes. He knew. He had no choice."

"Really, no choice?" I haven't even met the guy and I'm not sure I like him.

"He told me later that he'd hoped we'd ban together

and overpower the vampire... Somehow find a way out."

Disgust crosses my face at the situation she's describing. How could've it gotten so bad, so fast?

As if sensing my unease in the facts laid out, she continues. "First, the creature took his eight year old daughter." Her words drive a spike through my heart. "When his wife tried to find her, against her mate's orders, she was abducted as well." A heavy sigh escapes her and she sags against the cold wall, exhaustion and defeat etched into her skin. "By then it was too late for little Pamela. She'd lost too much blood to Cecil's addiction and couldn't bounce back." She motions to the pitcher, with the strange lime-lemon tasting water. "We found out about the blood replenishing additives later."

Power floods my limbs at her mention of the drink. I gesture with my cup. "What's in it?"

"I don't know for sure. We grow the plants out back at the vampire's direction. But he won't let us give them to Cliff and Kristin, our alphas." Sadness crosses her face. "My sister, Jennifer, was killed when she tried to sneak the herbs to them. Cecil keeps them chained and weak for a reason. I think together they would eventually overpower him. Their draining is very specific; they aren't *used* at the main house, but depleted here in the cells. He makes sure they remain on the cusp of death."

The return of my strength encourages me to test the chains binding me to the wall. A slight tug loosens their hold in the stone, confirming my suspicions. The water is working on me the same way it would work for Cliff and Kristin. In ten minutes I'm back to normal, like my blood loss never happened.

Raine reaches out a hand and touches my forehead. "Your gash, from the fight—it's gone already." Confusion mars her features. "It would normally take hours after that much blood loss to heal perfectly, even with the herbal-infused water." She gasps and hope lights her eyes. "Oh my God. Are you an alpha? That's the only thing that would explain it."

I nod, staring deep into her eyes. "Yes, I am." I wrap the chains around my fists. "You know what that means, don't you?"

"What?"

I rip the chains from the walls and stand. "I'm going to get us the hell out of here and find a way to save everyone."

Raine's hand flies to her throat, her mind whirring behind her startled eyes. "You've got to get out quick. Before he checks on you." She scuttles toward the door, gesturing me to follow. "I'll show you through a back door they can't see from the house." She checks the watch on her wrist. "You've got very little leeway until he'll come to test your recovery time. If he suspected you were an alpha he never would have ordered the enhanced water."

"You're coming with me, right?" We glance up and down the hall and then scurry along the deserted passageway to a dimly lit staircase leading up.

"No, I can't," she whispers. "If he suspects I've helped you he'll kill one of my packmates in retaliation." We make our way to the top and down another dark hallway leading to a back door. "Each of us knows the penalty for running when we're let out to work and attract other Weres to his net." She faces me at the threshold, rising up to kiss me lightly on the mouth. "I'm so sorry I got you into this. You're our only hope. Get out and find help. Even the local police if you have to—anyone!"

A grim expression settles on my face. "I won't let you down. No matter what."

A sound from the front of the building draws Raine around. "You don't have much time. He will follow your scent trail. He'll come after you even outside the property. I've seen him do it to non-pack wolves before." She grabs me and kisses me, desperation seeping from her pores like cheap cologne. "Be careful."

Without another word, she slinks down the passage while I creep silently out the backdoor. The light from the moon reveals I'm near the rear of the property, the outline of the mansion looming way too close for comfort. I angle deep into the woods, hoping to come out near my jeep parked along the main road.

My beating heart thunders in my ears as I slip between the tree trunks, trying my best to make as little noise as possible. The urge to run as a wolf burns under my skin, tempting me to succumb to the raw fear pulsing through my veins to let the animal side take control of my safety. A shout sounds far behind me and it takes every ounce of restraint I possess to maintain human shape. I can't waste time changing back to a human and I can't drive in furry form.

Increasing my pace, I emerge from the dense growth, unsure if I'm being pursued or if my overactive imagination fears the worst.

Unwilling to waste any time finding out, I hightail it to my jeep. I'm seized by a momentary blinding panic when I realize my wallet, keys, and cell phone are missing from my pockets. What the hell was I thinking? That they wouldn't search me and take my stuff? Sure, let's kidnap someone and give them access to their car keys and cell phone, just to make things interesting.

Fucking idiot!

Relief surges through me as I recall the backup set. I lost my keys on a job site and had the foresight to stash a second set in the spare tire hanging on the back.

I dig them out and scramble into the jeep, turning the engine over—the noise shockingly loud in the quiet night. I pull away from the side of the road, returning the way I came, when a figure steps out from the trees directly into the jeep's path.

I fumble in the darkness and turn on the headlights, flooding the night with the harsh blue-white of the halogen bulbs. The angry face of Cecil, fangs extended, fury etched in every feature, leaps into clarity, pulling a startled shriek from me.

Instead of swerving, I punch the gas, heading straight for the son of a bitch. Hatred burns in his maddened gaze as he jumps to the side, just missing my front left fender. I floor it, getting the heck out as fast as I can, my pulse drumming loudly through my ears.

Glancing constantly in the rearview mirror, I sigh in

relief when I reach Route 7.

Holy shit. What have I gotten myself into?

It's only when I cross the city limits into Leesburg does it hit me: that bloodsucker has my wallet and knows where I live.

CHAPTER SEVEN

I stop at my new apartment, throwing every piece of clothing and anything lying around into bags—including a handful of cash, my bills, and my passport—eager to get back on the road. How much time do I have? Where can I go? Leesburg is close to the West Virginia border. Maybe I'll find a pack there willing to help.

Once again, having no way to connect with fellow werewolves through an organized system leaves me at a disadvantage.

You're going to beat that dead horse over and over, aren't you? You could call Romeo and ask for help, you arrogant bastard.

Good point. And I will call him. When it's broad daylight, where there's no fear of some bloodsucking nightmare grabbing me in the dark, *and* after I buy a new phone. This is one of those few times in my life I see the need for a paper address book.

Yeah, if you could find a working payphone.

Some days, technology sucks.

I drive through what remains of the night, adrenaline and fear pushing me hard. I stop in Charlestown, West Virginia near the Maryland border and check into a cheap roadside motel using the scrunched cash I found in my glove compartment and on the dresser in my apartment. I race into the rented room and immediately check all points of entry and exit—two windows near the door are the only way out. No windows line the back. Man, from now on I'm planning better. One lost wallet and cell phone and I'm up shit's creek.

Yeah, well how often do people get into situations involving a werewolf blood addicted vampire?

God, I have no idea. I hope never again. Once in a lifetime is enough for me. Cold reality hits me like a ton of bricks—I need to figure out a way to help those people. What the hell am I going to do?

How do vampires track prey? Is it scent? Do I need to worry when I'm in a car? Could that son of a bitch track my electronic accounts and know when I access money at my bank?

Paranoia reigns king for about ten minutes, reducing me from a calm collected alpha to a scared young man who hasn't had much responsibility yet in life. I pace the thin, worn carpet of the small space and try to calm my racing heart.

I've got a folder containing bill statements from my apartment. So, I'll be able to call banks and such using the phone on the nightstand in the morning, requesting all new numbers and cards. That should slow down any cyber tracking, right? Suddenly, I wish I'd paid more attention to those cop shows Lori liked. I'm floundering, unsure what to do or where to turn.

There's nothing more to be done tonight. I take a shower, scrubbing the last trace of vampire stench from my skin, and slip on fresh clothes—planning to lie down fully clothed, just in case.

When the remaining fear and nervousness fueling me for the last few hours fades to nothing, sheer exhaustion envelops me. I open the drapes, allowing rays from the rising sun into the room to chase away the shadows. I settle on the bed, facing the light, letting its warmth grant me solace as I drift off to sleep.

I jolt awake at noon when the phone rings.

"You missed check out time, sir. It was at eleven."

"Are you fucking kidding me? I checked in less than six hours ago."

"Oh, terribly sorry, sir. I'm the day shift. I had no idea when you arrived."

"Yeah, well, I'm not leaving yet. I'll pay for a late check-out if I have to."

"Yes, sir."

I hang up the phone and stretch, grateful for the wakeup call even if it wasn't intended as one. I grab my bill folder and start making calls to have new cards issued. Too tense and afraid to remain in one spot for long, I pick a Maryland hotel from the phone book to have the new cards overnighted to.

Next, I need cash. My stomach growls at the reminder I used the last of my money to pay for this place. I climb into my jeep and drive to the local branch address for my bank. Losing every scrap of plastic to identify me is a pain in the ass, but thanks to my passport and bank statements I'm able to prove who I am, getting a much needed cash advance—which will hopefully make me harder to track.

I leave feeling a wash of relief cascade over me. The bank will overnight a new debit card to my next hotel. The wad of cash in my pocket feels reassuring, but I'm still in a tight spot.

Yes, and let's add in the fact you just withdrew money from your account, idiot.

Dammit! Will this guy really come after me?

Oh, gee, let's see... you discovered his illegal blood brothel were he sells captive werewolves to any vampire willing to pay. I'd say you're pretty screwed.

A grunt of frustration leaves me as I try to block the annoying voice in my head. What if I went to the local police? A recounting of yesterday's events isn't something any sane cop would believe. They'd probably lock me up as crazy, to boot.

Could I spin the story differently—like human trafficking—and get someone to listen? Only one way to find out.

I need a phone. A sign for a mall comes into view and I head there, hoping to find a wireless store for my carrier. Could Cecil track my calls on a new phone? Relaying my fears for identity theft to the sales rep at the store, he convinces me to just get a whole new number.

Breathing a sigh of relief, I get a new cell and a new number. Alone in my jeep once more, I do a search on my new smartphone for the nearest state park. If there are Weres in the area, I might get a whiff of their trail in a large expanse of woods. It's a long shot but I've got to try.

Nagging unease slides down my spine as I drive the highway toward Little Bennett Regional Park. I reach for my phone once more, determined to at least *attempt* contacting my old pack for help. I call Elsa, reasoning my chances of getting information out of her are greater than if I go through Romeo. She answers on the third ring.

"Who is this and how did you get my cell number?"

"Elsa, it's me, Jon."

"Jon? Where are you? I've been worried sick."

Yeah, so worried she didn't even try calling me during the last month. "I returned to Virginia, but not my home town. A place much farther north. I've got a job and a place to live."

"I'm not so sure that's a smart place for you to be, but you're on your own now. You left quite a mess here to contend with."

I wince at her unspoken implications. "I'm not going to apologize for what I did to Kotsana."

A snort sounds at the end of the line. "No, I guess I wasn't expecting you to." She sighs. "What do you need, Jon? I have a feeling you'd only call if there was a reason."

The exit for the park appears and I take the next turn. "I ran into a really bad situation with the local pack."

She chuckles. "They don't want a young hotheaded alpha joining their ranks? Big surprise."

I squelch the desire to defend myself. I never knew she thought of me that way. "No. I discovered the pack is being held hostage by a vampire with a Were blood addiction. He sells their bodies and blood to visiting vampires."

"That's horrible! Their alphas should have had no trouble containing the vampire. Two alphas against one vamp are usually enough."

"Not when they hold your daughter hostage and then drain you to near death before killing her."

"Oh God, that poor girl." She's silent for a moment and I wonder if Romeo is listening to both sides of the conversation. "I'm sorry, but there's nothing we can do."

Anger boils inside me at her quick self-interested response. "Cannot or will not?"

"Excuse me?"

"You and the pack could help, but you won't. Isn't that more accurate?"

Her voice sounds sad, almost resigned. "I may not be happy with the individual nature of each pack and their masters, but it's how we live. Survival of the fittest, just like in the wild."

I take one last turn, directly into the public area and maneuver to a vacant lot. "We aren't wild animals. No matter what we gain from our wolf halves we are still human. Geez, Elsa, even humans look out for each other."

"It's not our fight. You can't expect us to risk our safety for them. We have our own people to protect."

"Whatever. Thanks for nothing." I disconnect the

call, disheartened it ended so badly. After stopping in the spot closest to the woods, I get out and take a deep breath, letting the feel of the forest seep into my bones.

The smells of old and new growth wraps around me. Rotting leaves, standing water, honeysuckle blossoms, and dark earth vie for prominence in the air. Slowly a calm energy eases into my veins. My inner beast stretches and pushes at my surface thoughts, eager to run. It's only mid-afternoon. I should be able to run for a few hours without worry of vampires coming after me. I didn't smell any humans on the mansion's grounds, so hopefully it's safe to assume Cecil doesn't have a stable of human servants he could sic after me at a moment's notice.

With a quick glance around, I strip and lock my clothes in the truck, then stash my keys in the spare tire. A light breeze moves the hair on my legs, offering a mild a respite to the choking humidity. I call my beast to the surface, a brief searing pain spilling over me as the transformation comes fast. I fall to the ground, my limbs altering as grey-tipped brown fur covers my skin. The subtle scents I noticed before now scream through my head. I take a moment to adjust, lifting my muzzle to the sky and savoring all the woods have to offer.

The scamper of a squirrel sounds to my right, urging me to give chase. I ignore the instinct and race off in the opposite direction, eager to search for a trace of my own kind. I've got to find help. Surely local werewolves would care what was happening over the state line? It makes sense that once Cecil's finished with this pack he'd be looking to replace them with whoever was close by.

After searching for hours, mental exhaustion creeps in. Only the setting sun spurs me back to the safety of my jeep. I didn't come across one trace of werewolf in the vast forest. I must have raced the almost six square miles at least three times. There's got to be a better way of finding another pack. Where would werewolves hang out socially in this portion of Maryland? Would they occasionally go to a local bar like we did in Manitoba?

I shake my head at my vain attempt in grasping straws. I'm screwed and I know it. Searching like this could take forever. If a smart animal doesn't want to be found, chances are you won't find it.

But what about an arrogant creature unafraid of being discovered by animals they deem below them in the pecking order? I recall hearing vampires are better organized than we are, and they have rules of conduct, too. What if I found one—would they help my cause or consider what Cecil was doing to be normal? I'd like to think if it were normal I would've heard about the barbaric practice of keeping a horde of Weres for a blood addiction.

Shrugging on my clothes, I slip into the cold truck and make my way out of the park.

Would searching for a vampire be any easier? There's only one way to find out. From what I was told, vampires like cities. Lots of victims to choose from in a confined territory. That settles it. I'll start right after I stay the night in the Maryland hotel and get my replacement cards tomorrow.

Looks like I'm headed to Washington DC to find me

a bloodsucker.

The irony of such a statement regarding a town full of politicians is not lost on me.

CHAPTER EIGHT

I wander our nation's capital for two days with no luck. Considering how jaded I've felt since discovering the supernatural world really does exist, I'm strangely disappointed our judicial system and governing body is not overrun by power hungry, undead creatures of the night. It would be convenient if we could blame our country's current problems on another species with a nefarious agenda.

Scouring the city in my wolf form late at night might not be the safest way to conduct a search, but it's the only way I can think to accurately trace a vampire in this overwhelming soup of exhaust, exotic foods, and depressing stench of under-washed bodies. Searching as a wolf also helps me keep on the lookout for Raine's master vamp should he still be out for my blood. Nothing beats a werewolf's nose as an early warning detection system for danger.

I trot across the National Mall, the large expanse of real estate between the Capital building and the Washington monument. Sparse trees and a moonless night offer the cover I need to explore the area undetected. Yesterday, I caught a hint of a vampire scent at the newly opened World War II Memorial and wanted to come back today to investigate further—the appearance of an animal control van last night deterred me from following the lingering vampire trail onto the streets.

Creeping along the ground, my jaw open to catch all the night's scents, I come across the same intriguing scent from yesterday, only this time it's fresher. Once I single out the trail from all the crisscrossing human odors, I follow it away from the new memorial.

The scent mingles tightly with a human male, and both meander along the edge of the mall, in the direction of the Smithsonian Castle.

Small side gardens dot the sidewalk along Jefferson Drive, each one designed to pull in the visitor to walk through the display. The pair stopped at each garden, lingering over every signpost dedicated to a person, cause, or battle. It's almost like the pair are sightseeing —in the dark.

A vampire sightseeing at night in our nation's capital?

I heard the really old ones could tolerate the sun a little, so depending on their aversion level, I guess it makes sense—albeit an odd sense, but whatever.

After an hour of tracking, I hit pay dirt. The trail leads to a dark corner of a small empty park, sculpted trees and manicured bushes hiding the vampire and her companion. A light breeze changes course, bringing the smell of sex and blood.

Could the man with this vampire be in danger? Is it forced blood taking like Raine and her pack have endured? Will the bloodsucker drain him dry and leave his corpse hidden in the bushes?

Unsure what to do, I slink forward on my belly, creeping quietly through the well-tended beds to get a view of what's going on. A small stone table bracketed by two curved benches appears. A woman sits on the table, her long flowing skirt rucked up to her hips, the edges of the fabric trailing toward the ground. The human man I scented earlier kneels between her thighs.

The pungent aroma of aroused female saturates the humid air, the musky scent laced with the subtle undertones of vampire. The woman must be the creature I've been tracking.

She's a slight woman with ample curves, full breasts exposed over her bra cups. One arm supports her on the table's surface while her free hand fondles one pert nipple. Two long strands of thin chain hang between her breasts, some type of large bead on each end. The teardrop-shaped beads sway with each moan of pleasure and gasp of breath.

The vampire's fingers tweak and tease one engorged peak while the man works between her legs. Her head lolls back, her long hair drifting past the edge of the stone surface. "I'm going to come, baby." The woman's pleasure rips through her body, igniting tiny convulsions as she swallows her groans behind closed lips.

"So controlled, Dria," the man says as he stands and

shoves down his pants with both hands. "I like to hear you scream."

These two are not new lovers, nor is this a passing man the vampire has picked up to seduce and abuse. I should stealthily back away and leave them to their privacy. But I'm drawn to the two lovers, excited by their chemistry.

The vampire angles her torso up, a look for pure desire on her face. "Then you'll have to try harder, won't you, dear?"

A slow chuckle bubbles from his throat, squashed the moment he plunges into her. "I'm always up for a challenge."

Her companion proceeds to fuck her thoroughly, drawing out her build up and playing her body like a fine instrument. Within minutes she's squirming and biting her lip to hold in her responses.

The vampire's lover leans over her reclined body and nuzzles her neck. His mouth latches onto her skin and she bucks, a loud moan escaping. He slides one hand down her supporting arm and lifts it from the table, easing her slowly to lie down. The added leverage allows him to drive deeper into her waiting body and she can't hold back her pleasure any longer.

Soft moans and groans pepper the night, interspersed with the couple's jagged breathing. I've never seen anything so hot in my life, but then again, I don't normally watch live couples doing it, either. The occasional porn, yes, but spying on real people? Nope, that's a new low even for me.

She may be the all-powerful vampire, but there's no

doubt their powers over each other during this sizzling encounter are equal.

A stab of jealousy pricks my heart. What they have is what I wanted with Lori—what I'd hoped to build with Raine. Both situations are hopeless now.

The man rises to resume his original standing position between her thighs, driving himself into her depths, a look of ecstasy twisting his features.

"Again, Dria. Bite me again. I want you to come a second time."

The pale skin of the vampire glows faintly in the dark, almost luminescent in contrast to the couple's dark clothing and her lover's tanned skin. Long unbound hair cascades down her slender back as she leans in, reaching toward her partner's neck. In a delicate kiss full of tenderness, she places her lips on his sweaty skin.

Pleasure spills across the man's visage, and his steadily pumping hips lose their rhythm, amping up to a frantic speed devoid of finesse.

"Yes!" the man shouts, his release upon him. Shudders ripple over his body as he continues to thrust. "Damn, that's fucking incredible."

The figure of the vampire convulses in pleasure and the two wrap their arms around each other, holding on to one another as their passion subsides.

"We have company, dear," the vampire says as she turns and looks directly at my hiding place. "Come on out, wolfy."

Panic seizes me and I run, bolting from the bushes into the night. The tinkling laughter of the vampire chases me, like a burn of shame down my spine.

What possessed me to stay and watch when their acts were obviously consensual and the man was not being harmed? Well, how was I to know she wasn't going to kill him, unless I stayed?

I run the three miles back to my jeep at East Potomac Park, never once stopping, worried I might be seen. As first contact goes, I could have done better. She knows someone is trailing her now and might worry I mean to harm her.

Damn. Running was pretty stupid.

No matter how embarrassed I am over being turned on while watching the two of them, the hard fact doesn't change that I need her. I need a vampire's help if I'm going to save Raine's pack. Recognizing her scent, I should be able to find where they are staying during the day and approach them like a normal person, rather than a pervert who watches them having smoking hot sex in a public park.

I sleep in my car. Again. At daybreak I hit the streets, doing a circle of the mall in human form and working my way outward to find the couple's scent. Now that I know exactly what I'm looking for I don't have to be in wolf form to follow it.

It takes about seven hours, but I finally track them to a hotel on E Street. With only the name "Dria" to go by, I don't think I can walk up and ask for a room number. The sun hasn't set, so I'm hoping that means the vampire will be in their room. I check into the hotel and shower, changing into clean clothes. I set the rest out to be laundered and head down to the hotel bar. It's located near the bank of elevators and will give me ample chance to intercept them when they leave for the evening—assuming they hadn't check out.

Damn, this plan has a lot of holes. What the hell am I going to say to her? *Please save my werewolf friend and her pack from an evil vampire?*

"I've always found the truth is the best place to start."

Startled out of my thoughts, I look up to see a gorgeous redhead in her mid twenties. She's dressed in a tight fitting pair of dark jeans and a low-cut black sleeveless blouse. A thin silver chain dangles down her neck, two gleaming drops of red, like blood, suspended from their ends—I recognize the necklace from last night.

A knowing smile curves her full lips. "Do you have a name, wolfman, or should I just call you 'Peeping-Tom'?"

CHAPTER NINE

My heart leaps into my throat and heat flushes my face. "I...uh...."

Her piercing green eyes pin me to my chair. "Name?"

The intense desire to answer her has my name spewing out of me. "Jonathan Stephen Winchester."

"Okay, Jonathan. Can I call you Jon?" I nod. "Last night can be forgiven; after all we were in a public place so it's our own damn fault. But following us to our hotel is just plain stupid." Her eyes narrow. "What are you after?"

The urge to tell this stranger every secret I've ever had wells up in me. The words tumble to the surface with no grace or setup on my part. "I need your help."

Surprise flits across her face. "Fine." She glances to the elevator banks. "We'll talk. Have you eaten yet?"

I shake my head.

"Come to our suite and Rafe will order room service." She looks around the crowded bar. "I'm sure whatever is so compelling to seek *me* out is not suitable to be discussed in public."

I nod and follow her retreating form to the elevators.

Well, you wanted to talk to a vampire. You got it, dumbass. Oh, and following her back to her room is really safe.

Dria snorts as the doors close, sealing us in.

Christ. Can vampires read minds? Man, if they can, I am so up shit's creek. Again.

"Stop projecting so loudly and I won't accidentally read your mind. You're so nervous it's like you're shouting your thoughts at me. Very hard to ignore."

My body jerks and I cast a glance at the small woman. "And how would I go about doing that?"

She smiles at me, reassuring. "First, relax. I'm not going to leap on you and drain you dry." She shrugs a shoulder and plays with a dangling glass drop on her necklace. "Not my style."

The elevator *bings* and the doors slide open. I trail the vampire down the hall. "Next, calm your racing mind. It will help you from mentally having to shout over your own conflicting thoughts—which is how you initially broadcasted the 'shouted' snippets to begin with."

My brain processes what she's saying, but staring at her denim-clad tight ass makes it very hard to implement. Clear my head. Umm... yeah...

Baseball. Football.

Washington is muggy, even in June.

Vampires kill people.

She stops in front of a set of double doors. "Good,"

she smiles at me while she slips her keycard in the lock. The light flashes green and she opens the door, pausing and reaching out to place a hand to my forearm. "Seriously though, you need to chill."

A tingle eases up my arm at her contact. It's gone the second she lets go and I'm left feeling better and slightly stupid over my worries.

"Rafe," she calls out. "I found him in the bar downstairs."

The narrow hall beyond the doorway opens to a large suite. The man from last night sits at a round table big enough to seat four, his laptop open in front of him.

He closes the computer and rises, extending a hand to me in greeting. "Hi, I'm Dria's husband, Rafe." He towers over me by at least four or five inches, looking like he outweighs me by twenty or more pounds, too. I shake his hand and do my best to hide my surprise that he's *her* husband. That equality feeling I glimpsed last night was not imagined, he really has a presence about him—quiet and stoic, but strong. And yet he's human.

"Jon." I reply. "Uh, nice to meet you?"

Rafe laughs, the sound tumbling out of him. "Jesus, you must have had some shitty run-ins with vampires."

My face tightens. He may think my reaction is funny, but these two are the unreal ones. A happy vampire with their loving partner? What world is this? Surely not the same one Raine's pack is kept for blood consumption in a secluded mansion and sold to any paying vamp who stops by. I feel a scowl forming and try my best to smooth out my expression.

"Oh dear. You've upset him, Rafe. Let the poor boy get some food in him first. I can hear his stomach growling from here."

Her husband places a large order for dinner and we sit awkwardly around the table waiting for it to arrive.

"You worked hard to find us," Dria says. "What is this about?"

This all feels surreal. Why is she so calm?

Probably because she can kill you or erase your mind at any time. That would make anyone pretty calm, don't you think?

I nervously glance from one to the other, ending my ping-ponging attention to settle on Dria.

Her voice comes out in a seductive whisper, "Tell us a little about yourself."

I stare into her deep green eyes and everything pours out. I tell her about being changed into a werewolf in my third year of college, my family living in southern Virginia who think I'm dead, the pack I lived with for a year in Manitoba and my recent departure.

I end with recent events, telling them how I found my way back to Virginia, started working, and became involved with Raine. I even explain the Were's duplicity and how she originally intended for me to become another werewolf used for blood.

"You've got to do something," I say. "There's a vampire who's captured a whole werewolf pack. He's addicted to their blood and rents them to visiting vampires in a brothel type of setting. It's horrible."

Our food arrives and Rafe and I dig in while Dria sips from a coffee mug. The couple stares at each other now and then, but remain creepily quiet during the meal. I wonder if they are participating in some form of silent communication, but can't think of a polite way to ask. These two definitely give a very insular vibe. Like it's them against the world, and the rest of us are on the outside looking in.

I shake my head when I remember why I'm here. Can one vampire really make a difference in that pack's situation? She's a tiny thing and those guys are mean as hell. An image of an enraged Cecil jumping out of the woods flashes back to my mind.

I finish my second steak and wait for the couple to speak. Not much more I can say to convince them, is there?

"I'm sorry, Jon," Dria begins. Rafe's face clouds with anger and he throws his napkin on his plate. "The vampire isn't breaking any laws. I can't stop him."

I jump up from my seat. "What the hell are you talking about? Not breaking any laws? He's imprisoned an entire group of people, keeps the alphas drained and chained, killed the couple's daughter, and basically serves every one of them to be raped and snacked on whenever he chooses. How is that possibly within the law?"

Her eyes soften and her voice comes out quiet. "He hasn't broken any *vampire* laws."

Rafe snorts, his anger palpable.

She ignores her husband's reaction. "Our laws are designed to protect vampires—and they're pretty vague. Nothing in them talks about werewolves. The focus is protecting the knowledge of vampire's existence from the human race and ensuring humans are not slaughtered."

Rafe rises from the table and walks to my side. "Dria, I don't like it. You know what he's describing isn't right. This is a horrible abuse of vampire power at the basest level."

She shrugs, turning her attention to the uncovered window. "It's still none of my business. No matter if I approve or not."

Rafe clears his throat. "Let's look at this hypothetically." He glances to me and then his wife, but the expression on her face clearly says she doesn't give a shit what we say. "This pack has how many members, Jon?"

"Not sure—a lot were killed. From Raine's description it sounds like there are at least fifteen werewolves being held."

He turns to his wife, his light blue eyes burning with agitation. "Dria, think of all the humans those werewolves were in contact with in their daily lives—at their jobs, in their neighborhoods, heck, maybe even who they are dating. *Those* people will miss them. They will raise red flags. It could very well explode into a huge stink."

Dria doesn't answer, but her face takes on a contemplative look as she stares out the window.

"I considered approaching the police with a human trafficking case," I say.

Rafe touches my arm and motions to the door. He walks me out into the hall and whispers, "Give what we've said to her time to sink in. Come back in two days."

Frustration at my own inability to do anything snaps my mouth shut. Can he really talk her into helping me? And why would he? I nod, grateful for his assistance and reluctantly leave.

I've said everything I can to convince her. There's no amount of money I could pay her that she couldn't just take from anyone if she wanted it. I've got to figure out something to offer this vampire for her help, some type of payment. Something she needs that would sway her. Question is, what do you offer a creature that can take whatever they want?

I pace the floor of my hotel room for hours, wondering what the options are. I need to talk to someone who knows more about the supernatural world than I do.

Romeo and Elsa, my old alphas, are the first to pop into my mind. Yes, they refused to put their pack at risk to help, but they might have answers.

I call the pack house, using the new cell I picked up in Maryland. Much to my relief it's Elsa who answers this line, too.

"Why are you calling this time, Jon?"

"I need some advice. Are you willing to hear me out?"

A sigh comes over the phone. "Okay, go ahead."

"A couple of questions first—why do vampires like werewolf blood so much, is it tastier or something?"

"Kind of, but my understanding is it's the power in our blood they want."

"Power?"

"Yeah, something about our blood is almost like an adrenaline rush of long-lasting strength. Like humans on PCP without the high and hallucinations."

"I see why that would be addicting."

"Not all vamps get addicted."

"Really? Why not?"

"Romeo and I talked about this once. We think it's akin to people who become addicts. For some, dependence comes quickly—whether it's cigarettes, caffeine, alcohol, drugs...whatever. They have an addictive personality or character flaw, I've even heard it called a genetic weakness. Makes them more susceptible to any kind of addiction. What if those same people become vampires? Wouldn't their addictive traits still be there?"

"So you're comparing a vampire drinking Were blood to drug addiction and how some people can become addicted to substances easier than others?"

"Yes, that's the closest analogy we've come up with. It's the only thing that explains why some vamps become ruled by their cravings and others don't."

"Interesting."

"Why? What are you planning, Jon?"

"You know what I'm doing—what you two refused to do. I'm trying to save a pack of wolves. Anything I learn about their predicament might help with finding a solution."

"Aside from finding a bigger, badder vamp to shut down the place, I don't know what you can do."

I have no idea if Dria is bigger or badder, but her

husband's deference and respect make me think she might be. "The real question, Elsa, is when you find that vamp, how do you persuade them to help?"

"Simple—offer something they don't have."

"You make it sound easy, but seriously, woman. How am I going to figure out what the powerful vampire doesn't already have?"

"Start with what you have to offer. Does she have a werewolf servant at her side?"

"A servant? Like a bellman or valet or something?"

"No, Jon. Vampires usually have an entourage. The more powerful, the more people surround them."

"Damn, this one only has one person with her."

"Are they traveling? Vamps might travel light to avoid being noticed."

The thought amuses me, vampires being inconspicuous and not bringing many "bags" with them. "She's here with her husband."

"Whoa. Did you say husband?"

"Yeah, why?"

"That means he's her bonded mate. I've known over two dozen vampires and only three had mates. The others had devoted servants, meaning plural. Depending on their relationship, she might not have any servants in order to keep him happy. He might be the jealous type."

Rafe didn't seem like the jealous type to me, but what the hell do I know from a few minutes in his company? It's not like I was stupid enough to hit on his wife, for crying out loud. Or that I'd want to given the fact she's happily married. And she could drain me dry on a whim. Yeah, that last thing really is the clincher.

We wrap up our call and I sit in the growing darkness of my hotel room. A vampire's servant. Would I be required to do her bidding and wear some stupid outfit like a chauffeur? Somehow, trailing behind her in a black suit would be even more humiliating then just doing her bidding.

Could I do it? Could I offer myself as a servant to this vampire to save werewolves I barely know? Would my sacrifice be worth their lives?

Now really, what the hell kind of choice is that? Soldiers die to protect our country every damn day. They do it for people they've never met and for rights and ideals that sometimes get distorted over time. But they do it nonetheless.

Back in Manitoba, I talked all the time about uniting wolves and creating a communication network. What would the purpose of such a network be if not to save packs from fates like the one Raine's is facing?

Resolve spills through me, clearing my brain for the first time in months. I have no idea what offering myself to Dria will bring me, but I know in my heart it's the right thing to do.

Now, I just have to convince that stubborn redhead and her husband they need me in their lives. I wonder if dressing in skimpy shorts and a tight t-shirt would do the trick or if I should be my loveable smartass self?

I'll go for smartass. I don't think her husband would appreciate the skimpy shorts.

CHAPTER TEN

Now that I have a plan, I'm reluctant to wait the full two days Rafe suggested. Instead, I trail the couple wherever they go the next day. Surprisingly, they continue to do the tourist thing, venturing outside their hotel and into museums once the worst part of the afternoon sun has past. When the museums close, the couple visits outdoor monuments, lingering again over the new World War II one.

I keep my distance, giving the couple privacy. But Dria knows I'm here, shooting a dirty look my way every hour, discovering my location no matter where I hide. Her advice to calm my surface thoughts seems to have helped my involuntary projection of what I'm thinking. Or at least, I assume it's helped since she hasn't tossed my inner thoughts back in my face.

That vampire is unnerving. From what I was told, her kind has to avoid the sun, but she seems to have no problem walking in summer daylight after four o'clock. Could she handle being out earlier or would she still be susceptible to damage at high noon?

The couple's love for each other is an almost tangible thing. People standing near them smile, and laughter spills from the two frequently. There's got to be more than a small shred of humanity left in this woman or she'd never be able to blend in with humans so easily—and I doubt her husband would be so devoted if she was a horrible creature.

Everyone has to have a few redeeming qualities, so even if she is shooting me death-ray looks she must be a decent person inside.

Or so you keep trying to convince yourself.

I'm not a monster just because I turn into a werewolf. At the root of who I am, I'm still me. Could this vampire be the same? And if that is the case, can I devote my life to serving her?

I watch the pair as they stroll hand and hand toward the long reflective pool outside the Lincoln memorial. The summer evening holds a refreshing breeze, chasing away a bit of the humidity the area is famous for. Dria and Rafe pass a bickering couple whose wandering toddler aims straight for the shallow water.

Dria notices the child and my body tenses. She wouldn't be contemplating taking that kid, would she? A chill steals over me as I see her attention zero in on the small body climbing the stone edge of the pool. A quick glance at the parents reveal they are unaware of the danger lurking so close to their little one.

The vampire drops her husband's hand. The small teetering body miscalculates on the wide edge of the pool, and plunges toward the dark surface of the water.

Instantly Dria crosses the distance between herself and the child.

I leap into action, drawing level with Rafe, while Dria calmly grasps the child and rights him before his parents notice. She twists and sits, quick as a wink, making it appear as if she was headed to the water's edge to take a seat the whole time.

A pent up breath I didn't know I was holding whooshes out. Heat burns my face as I realize I immediately thought the worst of the vampire. Like she'd be bold or stupid enough to grab a child to feast upon.

Rafe's low chuckle has me spinning to face him. "You should see your face. Fucking hysterical. Did you really think she meant the child harm?"

Shame courses through me. "I... uh..."

He nods his head in the direction of Dria. "My wife is very old. She doesn't need much blood to survive." Rafe stares me in the eye. There's a hardness to him I hadn't seen before. "And if you think she'd ever harm a child then you should never have asked her for help."

The tension coiling in me eases out. "You're right. I'm being an idiot." I rub my hand over my face. "I'm exhausted and have been running for days. It's been almost a week since I escaped the mansion. I don't know if the wolves I left behind are alive or dead."

When the parents come to retrieve their child, Dria dips her chin in greeting, as if nothing is amiss and the toddler didn't almost fall in while they were distracted.

"If he's addicted," Rafe says, "he won't kill them. They're too valuable."

I nod, not really reassured by his assessment but unable to prove him wrong.

Dria saunters to us, her face guarded. "You certainly are a determined son of a bitch aren't you?"

I jam my hands into my pockets, unsure of my decided course to offer myself to her, even though it's the only option I've got. "I have a proposition for you."

Her deep green eyes trail down my body. "I bet you do." Rafe clears his throat. Dria's face lights up with a cheeky smile. "I was just teasing him, love."

"Hear the boy out."

My spine stiffens at his words. Boy? I'm twenty-one. Hardly a boy. Then again, next to the older man's obvious fifteen years on me, I'll let it slide.

The people visiting the pool wander off as the last of the late afternoon light fades. We're not alone by any means, but no one stands close, either. I guess this is as safe a place as any to voice my concept.

Only one tiny hitch I need to clear up first. "You're not addicted to Were blood, are you?"

A pensive look crosses the vampire's face. "No. I don't suffer from such a weakness." Her eyes turn calculating. "Were you worried if I did agree to help I might try to take the place of this ruling vamp and seize his captive pack for my own needs?" Anger colors her tone and fear grips my heart at the rage I see boiling in her eyes.

Her misunderstanding was not my reason for asking—I was more worried she'd feast on me and kill me by accident—but damned if my line of questioning doesn't sound suspicious of me in hindsight.

"No! I swear that thought hadn't occurred to me." I look from one to the other, noting doubt clearly on Dria's face and amusement on Rafe's. "Couldn't you just look inside my head and clarify I didn't intend what you inferred?"

Dria glances into my eyes. Her face sets in a hard mask and she whirls away, "Get rid of this fool."

Crap! I stepped in it again. And this time I wasn't even trying.

A loud sigh escapes Rafe. "Damn, you really need to think before you speak. I almost had her convinced it was the right thing to do."

"What the hell did I say wrong?"

"Well, furball, you managed to insult her three times in less than five minutes." He nods toward the pool. "First, you briefly entertained the thought that she might snack on that family's child." The expression on his face clearly proclaims he thinks I'm an idiot. "Then you ask if she's an addict, even though she showed no interest in drinking from you. And now you practically accuse her of slipping into people's heads whenever the fancy strikes her." He stares where his wife went to sit on a park bench.

"But didn't she read my mind in the elevator? Isn't it a common thing for vampires?"

"No—and not the way you think." At my look of confusion he continues, "Okay, in the elevator you were projecting, like she said. She didn't have to attempt to read your mind so much as you made your thoughts clear as a bell to anyone sensitive enough to hear them. Most vampires don't go around poking in other supernatural's heads. It takes effort on their part to do so and the action is considered exceptionally rude. In some cases, with strong mental shielding, extra skill and strength must be used to read thoughts, which can be detectable to the person the vampire is trying to read. With such risk of discovery, the ability is used discriminately."

"Oh." Hope deflates out of me. "I've essentially called her a pedophile blood-drinker, an addict, and insulted her honor as a vampire. Nice." I shove my hands in my pockets. "Usually it takes more of an effort to score so hugely as an ass."

Rafe's hand comes down on my shoulder. "Don't give up. If saving that pack matters to you don't let a few ruffled feathers thwart your task."

Thwart? How old *is* this guy? Who the hell talks like that? I mentally brace myself. He's right, dammit. No matter what I think of myself and my actions, I've got to go through with my plan.

I stride across the gravel and kneel at the vampire's feet. Being submissive doesn't come naturally to me and I have to rein in every impulse I have to stare her straight in the face. Through herculean effort, I avoid looking directly at the redhead and say, "I'm sorry about my behavior tonight. It doesn't change the fact that I need your help. I can't fight this vampire on my own and I haven't found any wolves to help me. You're the only option left."

"Hmmph." Her breath huffs out in annoyance. "Not much of an option since I already said *no*."

Rafe wanders over and sits next to her, snaking an

arm around her waist—making sure I understand they are a package deal. Well duh, they are married.

I steel my resolve and get to the difficult part. "What if I offer you something you couldn't resist?"

I chance a glance at her face and see her intense eyes narrow at me in speculation. "And what could you offer that I need?"

"A vampire servant with werewolf blood. Someone who willingly donates when you need to increase your strength."

A small gasp escapes her. "You don't know what you're offering."

I look up, boldly meeting her gaze. "Yes. Yes, I do. I'm offering my life in exchange for Raine's pack. No matter how you cut it, those are good numbers: one life for fifteen."

Her voice softens with a gentleness I haven't heard from her. "You aren't simply offering your life. The bond can affect you. You might very well lose your sense of self."

Rafe's gaze turns calculating, not angry or jealous like I feared. "He's thought about this long and hard, haven't you, Jon?"

I nod.

"He knows what he wants, Dria. He wants your help and he's willing to risk his future for it."

Dria stands and walks past me. "Let me think on it."

I bolt to my feet and grasp her hand. "There isn't time. I need to get them out and stop him before he captures more wolves."

She hesitates and looks to her husband. They are

both silent for a moment before she nods. "I'll do it. I'll help. But we need a plan."

Elation surges through me, the rush so intense my vision fades for a moment. "His place is about ninety minutes away. We could end all of this madness tonight."

"No. We strike tomorrow. Let's check out of the hotel and find a place as close as we can without alerting him. I have an idea on how to proceed."

CHAPTER ELEVEN

After a late dinner, we pack and drive our two separate vehicles to Middleburg, where the property was indicated on a map, not Purcellville like I thought. All those twists and turns when I followed Raine wound up leading to the outskirts of where many remote palatial estates lie, quite common in the affluential area.

The three of us check into the closest motel, which is still a ways from the vampire's location, and then met in the couple's room to discuss a plan. Dria refuses to visit the mansion tonight, even to case the grounds. She didn't want to risk Cecil getting a hint of what was to come. We discuss arriving at his place the next night, dressed like we're going to a party—well, she'll be dressed anyway. I'll be going in wolf form so he doesn't recognize me.

After a brief trip to a local pet store to buy myself an expensive collar, I spend the next day sleeping. According to Dria it will be the only clothing piece I need to look like a well-kept vampire servant in his werewolf form.

We meet again in the couple's room to go over details and annoyance vibrates off the vamp's husband. The plan dictates that Rafe will stay at the hotel. For Dria's ruse of being an addict to work, she stresses arriving with only a "pet" would appear more believable. He grumbled a lot last night but seems more agitated now that we're leaving soon.

My nerves get the best of me, driving me to pace in their small hotel room while they stare daggers at one another. It's almost nine and we should be getting on the road. Dria clears her throat, drawing my attention to her expression, one reddish eyebrow raised in expectation.

The young-looking vampire holds a knife over her wrist and my stomach clenches over the next stage of her plan. "I don't understand this part. Why do I need to drink your blood?"

"You've met this bastard, right?" she asks. I nod, still unsure of how her blood will change that simple fact. "Got right up and personal with him—and he and his cronies drank from you?"

"Yeah, so?"

"He'll recognize your scent, even in wolf form."

My blood freezes as a thought occurs to me. "Could he 'call' me to him against my will or anything like that?" I heard about that once from the Weres in Canada.

"Don't you think if he could, he would've by now? You did say he went after you at your apartment, right?"

Chagrinned at the obvious answer, my panic dulls a

little. "Okay, good point. I don't know for sure if he went to my apartment, Raine just stressed that he had gone after escaped wolves before. How will your blood help?"

"Once you drink a few sips, you are marked as mine. The essence of my blood mixes with yours, slightly changing the underlying blood scent—not a lot, but enough to mask you from him in your animal form. He won't be looking too closely for danger in a visiting vampire's kept werewolf."

"Is my drinking of your blood what will make me your servant?"

"No. If I fed on you repeatedly or once very deeply *and* allowed you to have my blood it would bind us, making you my servant, but even then the bond must be renewed monthly to stay strong. Casual blood donation within a seethe would make you one of the seethe's companions, not my servant."

"Seethe?"

She smiles. "Forgive me, a 'seethe' is a vampire family."

I nod, only slightly freaked out by the whole concept.

"It's okay, Jon. I realize this is all new terminology for you. A companion is under the protection of the seethe even if they aren't blood-bonded to any vampire in particular. Anyone else a vampire feeds from is classified as a donor, and has no protection."

Rafe chimes in, "There is an exception, a way around the rules, if you will. If a person is blood marked, like Dria plans to do with you, they are considered off limits, even if they aren't technically a servant in your seethe."

This crap is getting confusing. "So I can be blood marked and not a companion or a servant?"

"Yes, the difference is who feeds from you—a companion can donate to everyone in the seethe. A servant is a private bond, continually strengthened with exclusivity over time, no other vamp can touch the person under penalty of death."

"Why is it important I understand all of this now? How does it relate to me taking your blood?"

Rafe looks to his wife and then me. "It has more to do with you understanding what you are getting yourself into."

"Does it really matter what we tell him?" Dria asks, discomfort clear in her voice. "Once I bite him it won't make a difference, will it?"

Rafe nods, not as affected as she is by the weight of what's bothering her.

"Why won't it make a difference?" I ask.

She stalks to me, death and beauty in a scary package. "Because when I bite you, you will lose your free will. The only thing you'll care about is what I want. Do you understand?"

It sounds like she's trying to talk me out of this. Like she isn't willing to hold up her end of the bargain because of the moral ramifications of possibly removing my freedom of choice.

"But I'm agreeing to it. That means I am accepting the consequences." In a show of good faith I take her hand holding the knife and lay it against her opposite wrist. "If this is what I need to do to hide from Cecil and help you take him down, then I'll do it. I trust you."

A sad smirk tilts up one corner of her full lips. "You shouldn't." She slices her wrist over a glass and bleeds into the red wine it contains. An ounce or so dribbles in before her cut heals before my eyes. "I'm a monster."

I reach for the glass. Staring at her guarded expression, I drink the blood mixed with wine. It coats my throat with a lingering taste of salt and copper pennies. "I may not have seen a lot of evil in my life." Strength seeps through my body, surprising me with its powerful jolt. "But there is no doubt in my mind I saw true evil in what Cecil is doing to those wolves. From what I've seen of you so far," I say with a saucy grin, "you're the lesser of two evils."

Dria's head lowers and she looks away. "Appearances are deceiving."

Heat sings through my veins and I feel like I could pick up a bus without straining. "Holy shit. Your blood packs a real wallop."

A sad smile ghosts across her face. "I know. Be careful while you adjust to it. And before you ask—yes, vampire blood can be addicting to the right type of person, too." Her eyes harden. "And there was a time when vampires were hunted and drained for it."

She goes from lighthearted and fun to scary and distant much too quickly for my tastes. I look to her husband, who only has eyes for her, watching her every movement with an intensity I've never seen among the over-sexed wolves.

Without another word, she heads into the

bathroom to change into her evening gown. When devising this plan, I'd explained the formal dress I witnessed the vampires wearing in the dining room, and every other detail I could remember. Dria said it reminded her of an old European blood brothel she'd been to centuries ago. She knew exactly how she should dress to be accepted, and even assured me a pet werewolf would fit right in with the perceived decadence.

"Get ready, wolfman," Rafe says. "We don't want you struggling to shift in the back of the rented Benz."

Wolfman, eh? Is that how he wants to play this? Cheeky bastard. Bet I could take his big muscle-bound ass in a heartbeat. Then again, that could be the vamp blood talking. He's got something lurking in his eyes when you look closely, and strangely, it reminds me of staring into the eyes of a live wolf. I nod, not trusting myself to speak, and retreat to the second bedroom.

I leave the door slightly ajar so I can open it in wolf form—only takes locking yourself in a room two or three times, and the subsequent replacing of the door with a new one later, to drive the habit into your brain. I attach the expensive studded collar to my neck, leaving the clasp on the last notch so the leather won't be too stifling. A collar. Jesus. Is this what I've come to?

Yup. And you asked for it buddy. Might as well quit your bitching and take it like a man.

I strip, putting the clothes in a bag so we can stow it in the back seat when I revert back to human at our departure. Once my tiny tasks are completed, I take a deep breath, centering myself.

The vampire blood coursing through my body feels exhilarating and I have a hunch the change will come on me faster than normal. The mere thought of running free in the woods calls my wolf to the surface with lightening speed. In the span of two heartbeats I'm forced to the floor, and fur washes over my altered shape. For the first time since I was attacked last year, there is no agony in the transformation. None at all.

I give my head a shake and marvel at the joy that washes through me at the lack of pain. A small yip of happiness erupts and I duck my head, embarrassed by the outburst. I wait a little bit, hoping Rafe and Dria didn't hear me, and then use my mouth to grab the handles of the duffle containing my clothes.

I trot into the main living area of the hotel suite, bag in mouth, to see Rafe pacing the floor. He turns to me with a stern look, raises one eyebrow and says, "You'll do." He glances over his shoulder, toward the room Dria is changing in, and then back to me. "Make sure she comes back okay or I'll go in and kill the whole lot of you, vamps and Weres alike." His eyes darken as he takes a step toward me. "Fire will wipe out this problem just as easily."

I drop the bag and my hackles rise. A low growl starts in my throat. What the hell? I thought this big bastard was on my side.

"Finding my attitude contradictory, are you?" The tall man shrugs. "First and foremost, I care only about the safety of my wife. Sure, I was the one who helped talk her into helping you, but I'll never forgive myself if you two are walking into something dangerous and I'm stuck back here, twiddling my damn thumbs."

Dria takes that moment to make her entrance, sweeping out of the adjoining room like a debutant entering her first ball. The black gown she's wearing hugs her ample curves, showcasing what nature gave her to its absolute best.

"Now, now, darling. Have faith in me." The smile on her mouth is coy and relaxed. "The day I can't handle a few misguided vampires is the day I give up to the sun for good."

She strolls across the room, attention focused on her husband. "Will you promise to remain behind?"

"Only if you promise to keep our connection open, no matter what. If you shut me out I'll snag Jon's jeep and be out there in ten minutes."

She stands on her tip toes and kisses his mouth with tenderness and possession. "Yes, dear."

Rafe doesn't look appeased, and stands with his arms crossed over his chest. "Every single second, Dria. Don't test me."

She nods in his direction, then motions with her head toward the door. "Let's go, Jon." She grabs a small purse off the table, and jangles the keys in one hand. "Grab your bag, too."

I scoop up the duffle in my jaws and trot after her disappearing form.

"Don't forget what I said, furball. Watch out for her or I'll kill you all."

I follow Dria to the sleek black Mercedes they rented.

She opens the back door for me to jump in. I angle my head at her to convey my disapproval over her suggestion, but jump inside when she clears her throat.

The back seat? Does she really think I'm going to sit here the whole trip? I drop the bag in the back, wait 'til she settles in the front, and then jump to the vacant passenger seat.

"Oh, all right. You can sit in the front." Her tone is light, like all of this is one big game. "But don't mess up the upholstery, this is a rental."

Damn, this is weird. Maybe I should have changed into a wolf when we got there. I'm not used to interacting with people while in wolf form.

The stunning vampire next to me reaches out a hand and ruffles the fur at my neck. "Don't you worry, we'll be fine." She smiles into the growing darkness while driving. "Until you learn to shield better, I don't even have to try and pick up your thoughts. It's like they are written in red neon over your head."

I snort loudly, dipping my head toward the dash. *Does that mean the other vampires can read my thoughts, too?*

"Good job! That was a deliberate projection on your part, wasn't it? The words came through loud and clear. If you want to tone down your internal musings so I can't pick them up so easily you'd do much better around the other vamps. So—shall we talk about what's going to go down when we get there?"

I concentrate on my agreement as "loudly" as I can, *Yes.*

"I've been to many blood brothels in the past. They

haven't been common for over a hundred years, so that tells me the guy running this setup is at least one hundred years undead. Not sure what prompted him to try something that's been outlawed for so long. Maybe he thinks no one will find him here in Virginia." She shakes her head. "Fool. He's calling way too much attention to himself."

She turns onto the highway and begins the short trip to Cecil's mansion. "First off, we're strolling right up like we own the place and deserve to be there. If I recognize anyone things will move faster than I'd like, meaning I will have to strike to end this mess and get out of there quickly. But if no one knows who I am, we should be good to mingle for a little bit and get a feel where all the wolves are so we can free them."

Knows who you are?

"Yup. You, my dear sweet wolfman, sniffed out yourself an ex-enforcer." At my lack of comment she continues. "I used to dole out justice for the Tribunal of Ancients, the vampire race's governing body. Usually they'd send someone like me after a rogue vamp—a vampire who kills indiscriminately or puts our species in danger with his or her actions."

And your husband is worried you might not come back?

"No, not really. He gets like that whenever he's not by my side during a fight. Can't blame him, I'd probably react the same way." She glances at me sideways and then returns hers eyes to the road to take the next turn. "You do realize I'm going to have to kill Cecil tonight, right? There's no way to cure someone this far gone."

As long as we can save the wolves I don't care how many vampires have to die.

"Present company excluded, of course, right?" She doesn't even look at me on that one. "We're not all as bad as he is, you know. Humans would hunt vampires down and kill us, like they almost did during the Spanish Inquisition. Poor witches got all the blame, but a lot of supernatural species were under fire during that crazy time."

We turn down back roads, slowing our pace to follow the speed limit. "Now, what I'll do with the visiting vampires who have called on Cecil while we're there... that I haven't decided yet." The look on her face becomes distant. "Kill them all or alter their minds? I'll have to see when I get there."

The casual tone she uses to announce the imminent demise of her own kind chills me to the bone. Wolves kill to eat or defend their pack and den, not simply because it needs to be done. How do I feel about aligning myself with a cold blooded killer?

"Did I seem so cold blooded when you spied on me making love to my husband?" Quiet fills the space between us. "Or when I saved that child from falling into the wading pool? You know, when you thought I was going to eat the toddler?" I duck my head and glance out the window.

"I may not be a mindless beast, but I never walk away from what needs to be done—no matter how heartless I must become to finish the job."

We travel in silence a few more minutes,

apprehension filling my gut. What have I done by agreeing to serve this woman? Have I stepped into more than I can handle?

"I'll need you to follow my lead when we get there. Act meek and subservient, don't make eye contact with Cecil or the other vampires. Can you do that?"

Yes.

We pull into the gravel drive, the apprehension from before swirling into a larger mass of fear. If we can't save these wolves tonight I don't know what else to do.

The large house comes into view, every window lit up like a huge party is taking place. Six other cars line the circular drive in front of the house.

Dria parks the car and leans toward me, lowering her voice. "We'll walk away from this fine, don't you worry." Surprisingly, she has no problem smiling while I sit here worried I'm going to puke. "You wondered who you agreed to serve?" The cold look I saw returns. "I am death. And no one escapes death."

CHAPTER TWELVE

Dria exits the vehicle, holding open the door for me to jump out. She wraps one delicate hand around the studded collar and whispers, "Don't leave my side tonight. It's the only way I can ensure your safety."

I nod once, conveying I understand. Will I be able to hold back if I see Raine in danger?

"If you don't, you run the risk of ruining the whole plan." She gives my collar a jerk and then releases. "Think on that long and hard, numb nuts. Those alpha tendencies can get in the way and destroy the whole pack if you're not careful. Don't make me regret agreeing to help."

We walk to the front door and Dria rings the bell. A young blond woman, skinny to the point of looking anorexic, answers the door, a bright, forced smile on her face.

"Welcome to the V V Inn. Please, come in."

Dria's back stiffens at the woman's words. The hand resting on my back fists in the fur. "Interesting name. May I ask where it came from?"

The skinny blonde shrugs, the smile on her face faltering. "I'm not sure. Cecil, the owner, said it means something to the vampire community." The young werewolf locks eyes with me, trying to convey something—what I'm not sure. Maybe it's simply a warning from one Were to another to get out while I can.

"Yes," Dria says with a strained smile. "I've heard of it before. Hadn't realized there was a... branch here in Virginia."

"I take it this is your first time here?"

Dria nods her head regally. "Yes, it is."

"My name is Tara, I can show you around."

Tara leads us into the large foyer with two formal rooms branching off both sides. Midway into the house an elaborate staircase winds upward, and further back, a hall leads to more rooms.

Tara waves to the right with her toothpick arm. "Inside you'll find the parlor, where guests mingle with the available Weres, selecting a partner if one has not been prearranged." Dria nods and steps forward to glance about the room. Sticking close to her side as instructed, I follow, and see more than I'd bargained for.

Several slim werewolves lounge on heavy leather furniture, their gazes empty and unfocused. How much of their minds have been ruined by the constant control Cecil exerts on them? Can they heal from such damage and live a normal life?

Rage boils under my skin and I start to shake, minimally at first with the shudders gradually increasing as I try and hold still. The alpha in me calls for revenge, and a red haze of violence colors my vision, urging me to leap and tear out the throats of the nearby vampires ogling the emaciated wolves.

The studded collar around my neck is painfully jerked by Dria, the hard edge of the stitched leather digging into my airway. I glance up at her to see she's eyeing the vampires in the room, ignoring me completely, but obviously aware of my distress.

One vampire selects a slender man in his early twenties. He picks up the delicate leash dangling from the Were's navy blue collar and leads the unresisting Were out of the room toward the stairs. He ignores us in passing, but Dria studies him carefully as they exit.

When he's gone, her bright green gaze lingers on every bloodsucker in the room, like she's trying to place their identity or memorizing their appearance for a later purpose. There's a calmness emanating from her that feels down right spooky. I wish we had talked about more of an actual plan than "follow my lead" before we got here.

Who am I kidding? I'm basically at her mercy however you cut it.

Wow. Talk about humbling.

A chill races up my spine and this time it has nothing to do with my impotent feelings of rage at my fellow Were's treatment. Who should be able to wield such power over others? Isn't there an old saying that absolute power corrupts absolutely?

Dria kneels by my side, a deadly smile on her face, and whispers in my ear. "There's always someone more powerful who can knock you off your perch—even if you're me. Never forget it and you don't have to worry about corruption. You'll be too afraid watching your own back."

Turning her private *tete ala tete* with me into a show of something else, she says in a louder voice, "Which one do you think I should pick, my dear? They all look a little... tired."

Before I decide what she expects me to do at her question, she stands, dismissing me as if we never spoke.

Tara senses the difference in Dria's appraising stare around the room and says, "We have one or two that might appeal to you better. You could talk to Cecil and arrange something."

A huge smile spreads across the redhead's features. "Meet Cecil? Why thank you, Tara. What a wonderful idea."

Tension slips from the blond Were, pleased she did something right in the growing tension. She leads us out of the room toward the back of the building. The disturbing sounds of a nearby feeding vampire and forced pleasure from a donor chase us down the hall, tightening my gut and fueling me with the urge to rip and maim.

Dria's hand fists in my fur again, and then softens, smoothing the raised hackles I can't control in my distress. Tara meanders down a long hall and stops in front of a shut door. She raps once and waits.

"Yes?" a male voice calls from within.

"I've got a new visitor who would like to speak with

you about selecting donors not in the lounge tonight."

"Come in."

Tara opens the door and steps back, her body language projecting she's eager to avoid being in the room with either party, if she can.

Dria steps through the doorway with her head held high, her mane of lush copper waves spilling down her back. A large desk occupies one end of the room, with a small sitting area in front of it. The vampire who chased me into the night a week ago stands behind the desk, a fake smile plastered on his face. He steps around the desk and motions with one arm for us to sit in one of the chairs.

"Welcome. Please, take a seat."

My shoulder brushes up against her thigh as Dria walks to a high-backed chair and sits.

"My name is Cecil and I'm the owner of the V V Inn." He settles across from Dria, crossing his legs. "Tara mentioned our current selection tonight didn't spark your interest." He glances at me with a flick of dismissal. "Surely, if your servant isn't enough to satisfy your need, you'd be content with whomever was willing, no?"

A coldness enters Dria tone. "That would assume your donors were willing, wouldn't it?"

Cecil sits straighter in his seat. "I resent your implication. Our donors are willing. Ask them."

Her calculating gaze narrows on the larger man, not a trace of fear or doubt evident in her. "We all know how easily agreement can be coerced, don't we?" Dria scoots to the edge of her seat and extends her hand to the flustered vampire. "Allow me to introduce myself, I'm Alexandria McAndrews."

Her hand hangs in the air as Cecil's mouth gapes and his pale skin whitens. "No... You can't be..." He shuts his mouth and shrinks into his chair. "What are you doing here?"

A vicious look of satisfaction crosses Dria's face before she speaks. "Ah, I see you recognize the name, do you not?"

"Are you the one they called 'Alexandria the Great'?"

Dria rises from her chair to stand over Cecil. "That depends on who you ask. By 'they', I take it you mean the Tribunal?" Cecil nods, his eyes tracking Dria's every minuscule movement. She looks around his office, then brings her eyes back to his flinching features. "Interesting set up you've got here. I wonder what *they* would think of it." She begins to pace in her agitation, back and forth in front of the tense vampire.

"I'm not breaking any laws," Cecil says, forced bravado coloring his tone. I can smell the stink of fear coming off him in waves. This is getting interesting. Why would her name and reputation scare him so much?

Dria whips around and points an accusing finger his way. "*You* are doing something far worse. You have imprisoned these wolves and manipulated their minds to do your bidding. You pimp them out in an old-style blood brothel and think no one will notice?" Her hand drops to her side as her chest heaves in anger. "You think hiding behind a technicality that the laws weren't written to include werewolves would save you?"

"Blood brothel? This is no such thing. The V V Inn has been around for over a century, perhaps you never heard of it? We're operating like we always have."

"Bullshit!" The tiny vampire cries and leaps across the space between them, toppling the chair backward and pinning the terrified vampire to the floor. "I run the *only* V V Inn, you disgrace of a vampire." Cecil's face collapses in horror. "Perhaps *you* should have done your research better, asshole."

Without warning Dria plunges her hand straight into his chest and tears out the vampire's bloody heart. A scream starts from Cecil but abruptly cuts off when his heart leaves his body. Dria tosses the organ over her shoulder and pulls up her skirt. She extracts a hunting knife strapped to her inner thigh.

My stomach revolts at the horror before me and I swallow bile, hoping I don't hurl. In a smooth practiced move, Dria severs Cecil's head from his body and lays it a few feet from his body. Removing the heart first prevented any arterial spray, but her right hand is coated with red all the way up her forearm.

I may be a werewolf, but I've never killed a vampire, or anyone else for that matter— animals I've hunted while a wolf don't count as murder in my eyes.

Holy shit. Just exactly what have I gotten myself into with this woman?

She calmly wipes her blade and sullied hand on the dead vampire's suit jacket before glancing my way. "Well, crap. I hadn't intended to kill the bastard so quickly tonight. That was until I heard what he called this place—then all my best intentions went out the window." She sighs once, the sound tired and bone-weary, striding toward the desk.

Dria picks up the phone, while I stare at the wet, sloppy heart at my feet, and dials a number. In a moment whomever she's calling picks up. "Rafe honey, I'm going to need you here after all. We've got quite a mess to clean up."

CHAPTER THIRTEEN

Dria hangs up the phone and focuses her keen gaze on me. "Well, Jon, do you have the courage to eat the heart of your enemy or do you plan on staring at it for a while?"

You've got to be fucking kidding me. She wants me to *eat* his freakin' heart?

"Yes, Jon. That's exactly what I want you to do. When you kill a vamp you have an opportunity to ingest some of his or her power. Eating his heart will be the best route for a werewolf. As a vampire, I'd drink his blood—drain him dry if I were looking for the power boost." Her nose curls up in disgust. "Which I'm not. This bastard smells ripe with all kinds of crazy and addiction. I'll never be *that* hungry again, thank you very much."

The fresh blood from the recent kill fills my head, as the disgusting suggestion to devour his heart twists my gut. In wolf form I've eaten an animal's internal organs without a second's pause. Why does the thought of complying with her suggestion leave me disgusted?

Maybe because the bastard was human at one point? After all, you'd never eat a wolf, would you?

"That would depend on how hungry you were." Her cold eyes offer no reassurances. "You may not ever be that hungry, Jon. It's a different time we live in than just one hundred years ago." Her stare hardens and her mouth thins into a firm line. "Do it. Now."

I lower my muzzle to the warm organ. The smell of blood and slaughtered flesh fills my head and constricts my throat.

"Don't let the thoughts linger in your mind and take hold. This is not a life or death decision. This is an alpha protecting those weaker than him—growing stronger to keep doing so."

I close my eyes, clamp my nostrils closed, and gulp down the heart in one bite, not bothering to chew. The slick mass slides to my stomach, sitting like a hard weight in my middle.

I open my eyes to see her watching me, perhaps wondering if I'll puke it up and make an ass out of myself.

"Good. The power surge will hit you as it digests. Gross, I know, but one day you'll thank me for it."

Somehow I seriously doubt that, but I keep my thoughts locked down tight, trying to avoid what she called my projecting.

Her head tilts to the side as her stare intensifies. "Good. You're getting better at calming your thoughts." She walks to my side and kneels. "We're going to have a rough couple of hours ahead of us, are you going to be able to handle it? Before you agree, let me tell you what's going to happen." Her hand reaches out and stokes my fur. "I can't 'cure' a vampire of their addiction." Her gaze drifts to the wall as her rhythmic petting soothes my jittery stomach. "There is a way I could alter their thoughts... but it won't change their long term addiction in the end. This means the worst cases will have to die—here, tonight."

She stands, her comforting touch vanishes, leaving me with a feeling of coldness in its absence.

"It won't be pretty. It may haunt your nightmares for years. But there is no other choice." She pats me once on the head. "I won't think less of you if you need to go to the car."

A low growl rumbles in my throat. I will not be hightailing it out of here because things turn difficult. I knew going in this wasn't going to be easy. If I'm honest with myself, there was really no other way to end the evil that resides in this house. But if I'd known I was going to have to eat a heart I might have balked at joining her.

Dria's lip turns up at one corner. "Okay, wolfman, you made your decision. If you change your mind later I won't hold it against you. Cold-blooded killing isn't for everyone, but I promise to make things quick."

Her delicate nose wrinkles as she glances back at the headless corpse. "Dammit. I will have to take a sip from him to ensure the killing is done swiftly." Showing none of the hesitation or inner turmoil I faced a few moments ago, she daintily leans over the body and dips two fingers in the pooling blood. She pops the stained digits into her mouth and licks them clean, her face twisting at the tainted taste.

"Ugh. I've definitely tasted better, that's for sure."

Dria rises and sits again on the vacant chair. She closes her eyes and in a moment her face appears relaxed and serene. After a few heart beats, she opens her eyes, catching me staring at her.

"His blood is in all the wolves here. Their blood is in all of the visiting vampires. It couldn't have been more perfect for what I need to do. I can *twist* the connection to suit my plans without ever having met the addicts." She glances at her watch. "Come, let's get this over with. Rafe will be here soon and I'd rather have this part behind us when he arrives."

She opens the office door, revealing a shocked Tara huddled in the hallway. "Something is different," she says, the fear leaving her voice as she ventures to stand. "My mind is starting to clear."

Dria nods. "Yes. The nightmare is over for your pack. Go to where Cecil imprisoned your alphas and free them. Give them the drink that restores their blood and strength." Tara nods, her eyes as big as saucers. "How many 'guests' came to the house tonight?"

"Five."

"Good. Gather every wolf you encounter to the large building out back. We'll be there when we can."

"What about the wolves upstairs already with vampires?"

Dria reaches out a hand and places it on Tara's arm. Instantly the woman quiets. "Don't you worry. I'll get them out."

Tara scurries toward the back of the house. Dria

watches her leave and strides toward the front entrance. Her high heels ring out across the wood with each step. In a moment we're in the main foyer, facing the first room Tara showed us. The lounge contains one vampire mingling with three wolves. Wolves that look like they are waking from a long sleep.

"Jon, take them outside and return to me."

The Weres look to me, and I swing my head to the front door. Without a word they move as one to the exit. The man sitting in the room is the one Cecil called Nathaniel last week, the one who tasted Raine against her will while the others watched.

Curiously, he doesn't move and doesn't speak as I herd the Weres outside. I pause on the threshold, the retreating Weres safely in front of me, and glance back to see what Dria will do.

"Close your eyes, Jon."

Before I have a chance to process the request, and decide to follow her command or ignore it, Nathaniel's head explodes, showering the room in blood and bits of gore. Horror and shock roll through me as I stare at the redheaded vampire.

Oh my God. What is this woman I've pledged myself to? Is she simply a vampire or something more? What is this unleashed power Dria wields?

"I told you not to look." She turns to face me. A calm detachment on her face. "Four more to go. Why don't you go grab your clothes from the car and assist me as a man? It will be easier for you to help the Weres upstairs."

Without giving her a gesture of understanding, I

race out the door, feeling as if the hounds of hell were on my heels. I never imagined a vampire could do such a thing to another of its kind and wonder why no one has mentioned it. Granted, we didn't talk about vampires a lot in Manitoba, but surely if all of them could kill like that there'd be fewer vampires in the world, right?

The heat of the night wraps around me as I crouch next to the rented car. The hushed crying and whispers of the wolves standing nearby reach me, pulling me out of my thoughts to the here and now.

I reach for the physical change, picturing my human form in my mind. Flesh dissolves around me as the bones and muscles re-knit in a wash of energy so fast that I'm returned to man in the blink of an eye.

I rise from the gravel and open the back door, withdrawing the bag and grabbing my clothes with a speed I've never possessed. I slide the T-shirt over my head, then pull on jeans, apprehensive to face not only what waits for me inside the blood brothel, but to come to grips with exactly how I'm managing to move and change form as fast as I am.

It's the vampire heart, you twit. Guess you're digesting it faster than you'd bargained for.

My stomach clenches at the thought, the urge to hurl and dispel the vampire heart raging through my system.

"Who are you and what's going on?"

I turn and see the three wolves from inside, huddled next to each other a dozen feet away.

"I'm friends with Raine and came to help." Firming

my resolve as I quiet my gut and return to the house. "Go care for your alphas. It will all be over soon."

I march up the steps, the picture of the exploding vampire head front and center in my thoughts. Will she kill them all the same way? Without even a fight? Is there honor in a battle that isn't fought but obliterated like a nuclear bomb?

Our government didn't stand and debate for years when they dropped the bomb on Japan, now did they? The only choice is usually the hardest to make.

Dria waits for me in the foyer, her head angled toward the stairs and what awaits us above. "Next time I tell you to close your eyes, listen."

I move to stand before her, meeting her green gaze without flinching. "If you can handle it, then so can I."

A sad smile curves her mouth. "You never forget your first massacre." Compassion spikes in her eyes for an instant before vanishing. "It will haunt you forever. I would have liked to spare you the pain."

"Being an alpha means I don't get to wear blinders when times are tough, right?"

"Yes, Jon."

"Well then, it's about time I face the world with my eyes wide open."

She nods and places a foot on the first stair. "There will be days you regret this decision. But, I understand." Dria looks over her shoulder and there's a sadness on her face. "What doesn't kill us makes us stronger."

CHAPTER FOURTEEN

The next five minutes shake the very foundation of my sanity. At each occupied bedroom we encounter, Dria has me usher the victimized Were out the door and down the hall, while the previously feasting vampire sits utterly still. Once the Were passes, she closes the door, leaving it slightly ajar, and stands in the hall while the wet splatter of the addicted vampire's head explodes in the room beyond.

It would all seem surreal and out of a movie if I wasn't smelling the gore and seeing the blood on the red stained walls when a door happens to swing open. By the third one the gorge in my stomach tries to force its way up my throat. I can't do this. I can't sit by and watch this mindless killing.

Dria's cooler hand rests on my arm as we travel toward the last room in the hall. "Steady, Jon. You can do this. Only one more to handle."

"Don't you mean 'slaughter'?" I try and pull my arm out of her grasp, but she holds firm. "For God's sake, you're not even giving them a chance to fight."

She leans in, her voice whispering near my ear. "Like they did to the wolves, Jon? These vampires captured their minds and held them captive while they raped and used them for their own twisted needs." Her breath tickles my neck and I shudder, torn between loathing and vengeance. "Revenge is never pretty and often leaves you empty. Focus on the lives we're saving and you'll get through this."

A quiet calmness fills me, but my soul screams. It seems wrong to kill anyone without a fight.

Dria releases my arm and stares into my eyes. "It is —in a perfect world. But ours is far from perfect. Remember what they told you happened to the daughter of the alphas?" I nod. "Save your mercy for children like her and do the hard task that needs to be done in her honor."

She's right, I know. But I never signed up for heartless, cold-blooded slaughter. I never dreamed her plan would include the quick execution of everyone responsible.

What did you think would happen? That the vampires would all promise not to abuse Weres again and everyone would be magically set free?

My own naiveté chokes me. Good God, what an idiot I am. I shake my head, trying to clear the bloody images from my mind. Worry creeps in when I realize who we haven't freed from these upstairs rooms. "We haven't come across Raine, yet."

The vampire's face takes on a faraway look. "Does she have short dark brown hair, skinny as a rail, and soulful blue eyes?"

In my mind's eye I think of the young Were, the woman who was able to resist Cecil's compulsion thanks to a spark between us, the dimple near her upturned mouth and the twinkle in her eyes. "Yeah, that sounds a little like Raine."

"Well then, you'll get your wish." She motions down the hall. "I'm pretty sure she's on the other side of the last door on the right."

"How do you know that?"

She moves stealthily down the carpet toward the last room. "That's a story for another day, wolfman."

Dria eases to one side of the door. Her green eyes seek out mine as her body tenses. "It's not going well in there. We need to get in there quick—it may already be too late."

Without another word from the vamped-out killer, she kicks open the door. The second man who attacked me last week, Thomas, lies naked on his side, his body wrapped around the unmoving form of Raine.

Another rush of adrenaline floods my body, promising a wicked crash when the danger is finally past. Fire surges through me with the desire to rip and tear the leech limb from limb. Raine's eyes are closed and her pale skin almost glows in the half-light of the bedroom.

"You're too late," Thomas calls from the bed. "I heard your... exterminating techniques a few minutes ago and knew my fate was sealed."

Dria steps into the room, her eyes locked on the vamp with the bloody mouth and not the ripped out throat of Raine on the bed. My God, we might be too late. The urge to rush forward and save her compels me forward, but the strong arm of the redheaded vampire bars my passage.

"Why kill her?" Dria asks. "She did nothing to you."

He ignores her and asks a question of his own, "I felt you in my mind, didn't I? I've never felt the presence of another vampire in my awareness. You were hard to miss."

My senses strain toward the girl on the bed. Is she truly gone or can we save her? I try and listen for her heart beat, but can't discern anything over my own pounding pulse.

"Shh..." Dria says, and the man on the bed goes silent. There's a frown on her face when she turns to me. "Jon, check to see if she still lives."

I stride past the redhead, watching Thomas the whole time. Will he leap on me and rip out my throat when I approach?

Once I reach the side of the bed I place two fingers on Raine's wrist, hoping for a response. Nothing. I lean down and rest my head on her chest, hoping, straining for some sign of life. Pain wells and grabs my heart, like it's being crushed in my chest. She's well and truly gone.

Anger and pain over her loss battle inside me. I want nothing more than to rip apart the vampire who did this to her, to feast on his flesh, and gorge on his blackened heart. As the muscles in my shoulders bunch and I prepare to leap, one thought holds me back. I judged Dria just moments ago, and yet I'm ready to do the same damn thing—kill and destroy an enemy who hasn't even lifted a finger toward me. Why is it he hasn't moved? What the hell is she doing to him? Reining in my primal urges for vengeance takes every ounce of will power and strength I gained from eating Cecil's heart.

"Why?" I ask him, my voice harsh with the devastation of losing Raine. "You hear us coming and you still didn't try and flee? You went after her instead."

The vampire stares at me silently, not moving a muscle, not twitching an eye. It's like he's frozen.

"What he has to say doesn't matter, Jon." Dria says. "If she's gone I can't bring her back and nothing he could add would make you feel better—it will probably make you feel worse." A hand lands on my shoulder, the touch light and reassuring. "Would you like to end him or shall I?"

Disgust coils in my gut and bile rises up my throat. I shake my head, afraid to speak and spew the hatred coiling inside me. I pull the limp form of Raine away from him, picking her up in my arms, and cover her nakedness with the bed sheet. Cradling her lifeless form to my chest, I turn and leave, letting my actions answer for me.

Halfway down the hall I hear the door close behind Dria and the distinct splatter I've come to recognize in the last few minutes as the quick and final death of another vampire.

Tears trickle unchecked across my face as I carry the dead woman down the stairs. Could we have saved her if we'd moved faster? Would she have lived if I hadn't trailed her back to the mansion last week? So many conflicting thoughts fight for dominance in my mind as one foot follows another and I painstakingly make my way to the rear of the house, where we told the other Weres to gather.

The weight of her body pulls on me mentally, but not physically. Her arms lay loose, one cradled to her body and the other dangling toward the ground. With each step, the burden of carrying her draws me into a pit of despair.

I failed this woman. I thought I could help, but in the end I was no match against an enemy who outnumbered me and had advantages of strength and experience.

If it wasn't for the more powerful vampire I'd stumbled upon, this whole pack would be dead—if not now than surely later as the years of their torment stretched on.

You did do something. You didn't turn your back on them like Romeo and Elsa. You found someone to help.

Yeah, and at what price? Raine is dead and I'll be serving the deadliest creature I've ever met. What if she gets tired of me? What if I make a wrong move? Could she dispose of me without a backward glance, like she did those vampires in the house? The noise of hushed voices reaches me as I make my way to the backyard.

A blurry glance reveals the rest of the werewolves have gathered outside. Two dirty forms huddle near the ground, several other packmates standing close to them. My guess would be the ones on the ground are the chained and drained alphas from this unlucky pack. At my slow approach, a few Weres turn in my direction.

"Raine!" The young wolf from the house, Tara, rushes to my side. "Is she...?"

The crushing weight of my failure shoves me to my knees, clasping the body of the slight werewolf to my chest as I descend. "I tried, Tara... I really tried."

"No!" she shouts, tears cascading down her face. She reaches to take her packmate's limp body from my arms, the sobs wracking her shoulders don't hinder her supernatural strength to support a woman her size. I release my hold on Raine's remains. My back bows and my head sags.

All this, for... what?

Was it worth it? You sell your soul to the devil and your potential mate lies dead?

Dria lays a hand on my shoulder. Her touch eases some of the despair coating my thoughts. "I'm no angel, that's true." I turn my head and stare into her glittering green eyes. "But I'm sure as hell not a soul-collecting devil, either."

My mouth opens to refute the betraying thoughts she read, but she pats my shoulder, stopping me. "It's okay, Jon. You're allowed to feel pain and grieve. If you didn't, I'd be worried about you—and the type of alpha you'd make without compassion." Her hand grips the fabric of my shirt and she gives a gentle tug. "Get up." I stoically rise to my feet, wanting nothing more than the ground to open and swallow me over Raine's loss—and my horrible failure at letting her die.

Dria's next words whip a light of fire through me.

"We're not done yet. Wipe your tears and let's get moving. There's more to do, whether you're ready for it or not."

CHAPTER FIFTEEN

"What?" The question leaks past my shock-parched lips, quiet enough to be more of a whisper. Fear squeezes my heart as my muscles tense. "You don't plan on...?" I trail off, afraid to voice my inner fear that she may not stop her killing spree with just the vampires.

"Worried I'll hurt the wolves?" she asks, a twinge of annoyance on her pale as porcelain face. "Now really, Jon. What kind of help would I be if I intended to kill the wolves? Anyone with some accelerant and a lighter could've done that ages ago by burning this whole place to the ground."

I turn to face her, confusion spilling out of me. "Well, then...?"

She reaches out one pale hand, cupping my cheek with a delicate touch. "I'm sorry I wasn't able to save Raine." Her eyes dart to the group of skinny huddled bodies outside of the building that held me hostage a week ago. "I plan on helping as many of the wolves as I can, trust me. I would've never accepted your offer otherwise."

She drops her hand and strides to the ragged pack of Weres. I trail behind her, unsure what she's got planned. She stops ten feet from a stooped man with matted hair and a scraggly beard, who huddles over the emaciated form of an equally dirty woman. Dria angles her head my way, her voice coming out low, for my ears only. "The night is not over, Jon. Not by a long shot. Sure, the worst of the hell is past, but we've got hours more ahead of us." Her eyes flick behind us to the empty mansion. "Rafe will be here soon. We'll be burning this place to the ground—he'll start on getting it prepped." She motions with her chin toward the couple. "I think those are the alphas. I need to talk with them before proceeding with the next stage of my plan." Her serious stare drills into mine. "I need you by my side. Are you up for it?"

Resolve stiffens my spine. I may not have been able to save Raine, but I will follow through with my promise to this deadly creature.

Her eyes sharpen while she stares at me. "Well?"

"You can count on me, Dria."

After a small nod she approaches the couple, crouching down to their level on the ground. "Are you the alphas of this pack?"

The man nods, his hand coming up to rest on his wife's shoulder. "Yes. I'm Cliff and this is my wife, Kristin. Are you the one responsible for the end of our hell?"

A Were rushes forward with two pitchers of water and another hands a cup to each of the shrunken alphas. Dria hesitates in answering, letting the two drink their fill before continuing the conversation.

The scent drifting up from the water tells me it contains the same additives that healed me after I was drained by Cecil and his fellow addicts. I doubt one pitcher will bring these two back to anything close to resembling good health, but it's a start in the right direction.

The sound of tires on gravel drifts to us from the side of the mansion, pulling the rag-tag group of victim's attention toward the noise. The tension spilling off a few of them has me stepping forward to reassure them. "It's not another vampire. The new arrival is a human here to help." I motion toward Dria. "Just like she is."

Cliff and Kristin manage to stand after drinking the entire pitcher, the proud bearing of their former leadership shining through the dirt and grime. Kristin steps forward first, her right hand extended in gratitude toward the vampire. "Thank you."

Dria steps back deferring the credit to me with a wave of her arm. "I never would have come if it wasn't for Jon. He's the one you need to thank."

Cliff steps up next to his wife. "From what the other Weres have reported, it's your strength and... skill, that saved us."

Dria looks uncomfortable at the gratitude and steers the conversation in another direction. "Cliff, we need to talk about your wolves."

The tall, thin man looks around at his tattered pack of skinny werewolves. "Yes? What about them?"

Rafe's approach from behind draws her focus away for a moment. The couple stares intently at one another for a moment, and then Rafe nods sharply. More of that silent communication I suspect is happening between the two, I bet. I'd like to know what the hell they were discussing.

Kristin speaks up, brushing her wildly unkempt and dirty hair from her eyes. "Is there something you wanted to say...Miss...?

Dria returns her attention to the alphas. "Please, call me Dria." She gestures toward the building behind the group, where the couple had been imprisoned for five long years. "Can we talk inside? It will be safer."

"Safer?" Cliff asks. "What more can happen to us?"

"My husband is here to set a fire in the mansion, to wipe out every trace of the vampire remains inside. We won't light it until the pack is gone, but I need to work with the survivors and my task will take time—and solitude."

Cliff glances to his wife, confusion and uncertainty marring both of their faces. After a brief moment they both nod. "You've proven your trust so far," he says. "We'll hear you out."

They turn as one, the group nearby parting to allow them passage, and the four of us make our way into the low, long building. Kristin's shoulders shudder when she crosses the threshold, but she keeps going, head held high.

There's a grouping of old furniture just past the entryway. We stand in the middle, all of us looking to the vampire to see what she has to say.

Dria's voice softens, the soothing tone cascading over my skin like a balm on a burn. "Your wolves' minds have been damaged by the extreme control Cecil held over them for so long."

Kristin's face crumbles and tears trickle down her cheeks. She refuses to hide her pain and meets Dria's stare head-on. "Are you suggesting their minds will never heal? That they will remain like this—shadows of themselves—for the rest of their lives?"

The redhead nods. "Yes. That is my fear. But, I can help them."

"How?" Cliff asks, disbelief and weariness prominent in his voice.

"I can fix the worst of his mind meddling, but it will take me time to repair so many. Perhaps almost an hour per person." She looks out the small window near the door, her face pinching with worry. "But..."

"Yes?"

"I won't be able to completely erase their memories for so long of a time frame. I might be able to... conceal... the worst of the atrocities done to them—but not all of it. Not without a lot more time than we have and a plausible cover story you'd want me to insert."

A harsh bark of sound rips from the concerned man. "Cover story? There is nothing we could contrive to explain this horrendous imprisonment." He hangs his head in frustration. "If I could go back in time and volunteer my life to save theirs, I would, without a second thought... but we're way past wishful thinking and have been for a very long time."

Mistrust colors the gaze of his crying wife. "Can we

trust her?" she asks, turning her imploring eyes to me, obviously uncaring of voicing her concerns in front of Dria. "Why would she help us?" She looks to Dria, her moist gaze holding a fierce resolve. "We don't know you. Vampires have never helped our kind before."

Dria stands and moves to the window, gazing at the lost souls standing near one another for comfort. "That's not entirely true. Vampires have stepped in to help other supernatural species in the past." She shrugs, as if our discussing her morality doesn't affect her. "Unfortunately, many more of us have stepped in to abuse them as well. I don't blame you for being wary."

The urge to do something wells inside me, and before I have a chance to think about what I'm saying, the words tumble out. "I vouch for her." Three heads whip around to stare at me. "She won't harm your wolves, or you. I swear it on my life."

Silence fills the small space for the span of a few heartbeats. Dria's expression holds one of surprise while the alpha's holds confusion.

"And why would your word matter?" Cliff asks. "This is the first time I've met you."

"Because I volunteered to be her vampire servant and I can read her mind through our bond." The lie spills out between us, Dria's eyes narrow at my blatant fabrication. Hell, there's no way they would know I'm not truly bonded to her yet, or what that bond may or may not share. At the couple's shocked expression I add, "Yeah, that's right. I volunteered my life to her—to save your pack. If you don't trust her, trust me. I stand by my words—she holds no ill will or plans to deceive you in her thoughts."

Cliff nods once and stands, extending his hand to me. I rise and clasp his skeletal grip in my own. "From one alpha to another. I will put my faith in you." He glances in Dria's direction. "And that means in her, too."

Dria walks to the couch and takes a seat. "Good. Glad that's cleared up. This is going to take a while." She looks to Kristin. "Can you bring the first Were in and I'll get started? You're all welcome to stay and watch, as long as you're quiet."

The hours tick by slowly, and the sun rises while she works. To everyone's surprise, the sun doesn't slow her down. Dria's pace is relentless. One after another she sits with each wolf, holding their hand in silence while she repairs the holes Cecil's forced compulsions created. She explained that she's slipping into their minds, the physical contact making it easier, and re-knitting the very fabric of their consciousness to make the savaged Weres whole again.

Rafe and the healed Weres have been busy while she works, removing anything of value from the house —including the car keys of all the vampires who drove here and the numerous stacks of cash locked away in Cecil's safe. Five years is a long time to be missing, and the group has no residences to go home to. The money will at least support them while the pack gets healthy and tries to pick up the pieces of their lives.

By the time Dria works on the tenth Were I visibly see her strength waning. None of the wolves here are strong enough to donate blood, so I step forward. Unsure how to proceed, I bare my wrist to her.

"Here, it looks like you need sustenance to continue."

Hunger lights her gaze, drawing her need closer to the surface. She shakes her head and tears her eyes from my pulsing wrist. "No. I'm fine."

"You're not. I can see you're getting tired, Dria. Why won't you drink from me?"

Anger replaces her obvious want and she lashes out, her voice sharp as a whip. "I am the master here. You don't tell me what I *need*." Her green gaze locks on mine as she issues a command I'm compelled to follow. "Leave us, wolfman. Check on Rafe."

CHAPTER SIXTEEN

Unable to resist her command, I walk slowly to the door. On the threshold I turn to her, biting out my words, "I *will* come back to check on you. Make no doubt about that."

She ignores me, her attention solely focused on the Were seated next to her.

I stride toward the mansion, shaking my head in frustration. Damn, that woman is stubborn. How good is her control that she can continue what she's doing and not attack the weres in hunger?

Rafe's deep voice pulls me from my thoughts. "Did she finally kick you out?" He smiles. "You lasted in there a lot longer than I would have guessed."

"Why? It's not like she needed me. She just ignored me most of the time."

He rubs a dusty hand over his hair, resting it on the back of his neck in exhaustion. "She doesn't normally let people watch what she does." He nods toward the building. "I wouldn't doubt she'll alter the alphas perception of exactly what they witnessed when she's done. Not the kind of thing she likes to get out."

"What kind of *thing* do you mean? That she helped people? Why would she want that to be a secret?"

He heads toward a nearby tree on the lawn and lowers himself to the ground, resting against the trunk. I follow, but remain standing, the energy coiling inside me from the vampire heart still fueling me, pushing me to act, urging me to *do* something.

"Vampire society is complicated, Jon. Her compassion could be viewed as a weakness and used against her by an enemy."

"Man, that's fucked up."

He nods, his head drifting to the bark in exhaustion. "You have no idea."

I look across the grass at the freed Weres wondering what will happen to them. "What's next? What will we do after Dria finishes?"

"We see the wolves off safely. I called ahead and booked five more rooms at our hotel. They can drive the liberated vampire cars and any valuables they find to the hotel. After that, it's up to them. Their alphas need to be the ones to direct their future, not us."

His words make sense, but I still have this feeling of foreboding inside me. "What about the fire you plan to light? We don't want it spreading to the woods."

He raises his head, bright blue eyes locking on me. "I soaked the surrounding trees with water from a hose, and the lawn. The fire will be controlled and called in. We just want everyone out of here first."

I pace, the uneasiness in me spreading. "Yeah, yeah, that all sounds good. But what about *us*? What happens with the three of us? Where do you two live? Do I move there with you?"

"Things will unfold as intended." His gaze loses focus for a moment, like his mind is elsewhere, then sharpens when he glances toward me. "We'll talk more. When she's sleeping."

"So she does sleep, eh? I wondered. What with the sun being out and she's still wandering around."

"I told you before. She's very old. Doesn't need much blood or much sleep. But the sun of high noon could still kill her if she sat in it long enough." He pushes himself up, tiredness drawing down his large frame. "I know my wife. She's going to need blood very soon, and her body will force a restorative sleep on her whether she wants it or not."

"I offered her my blood. She refused."

His spine straightens at my words. "Dammit. She refused you? I worried she'd get a pang of consciousness."

"What does that mean?"

He shakes his head, refusing to elaborate more. "We'll talk later—like I said, when she's sleeping. Let's get the wolves into the cars and out of here."

By nine a.m. Dria is done. All the pack-owned vehicles, like Raine's, and the visiting vampire's luxury cars leave the property. The wolves will travel to the hotel where food and warm beds await them. One of them gathered as much of the special herbs as they could find, with plans of having everyone drink their fill of the healing concoction later.

Dria's exhaustion is apparent to anyone paying attention. She walks a little slower and doesn't glance our way as she staggers to the rented Benz. Without a word, she opens the back door and crawls inside, lying in the shadowed interior. Rafe and I check the accelerant placements carefully, making sure the headless vampire remains are well-covered for maximum temperature and destruction.

"Won't the firemen find their decapitated skeletons when they send in a fire investigator?"

"Nope," Rafe says. "Once the sun hits their bones, the remains will turn to dust."

"Why not just drag their bodies out to burn and save the house?"

"Too much evil has been done in that house."

A snort of disbelief comes from me. Does this guy really believe all that crap?

He looks at me sideways. "You think I'm joking. No amount of cleansing could save it and whoever lived in it afterwards would suffer."

"Seriously? That sounds like bullshit to me."

"Think what you want, furball. I've seen it in the past. It's best to burn it and hope the next structure built here doesn't occupy the same space. Just as good feelings can permeate the atmosphere of holy structures and scared spaces, same can be said about places were great evil has occurred."

"Whatever, man."

"Come on—surely you must be open to some kind of belief. After all, if you'd been told werewolves and vampires were real before your attack you never would have believed it, right?"

"Yeah, I guess so."

"Same thing applies here. Witches and witchcraft, wizards and fae, demons and even more shapeshifting creatures from various mythology than you ever guessed, all roam this earth—why not good and evil?"

"I never thought about it too closely." An uncomfortableness settles inside me. "Are those things true? Do all those... species really exist?"

"Yup. Humans have never been the top predator. We just like to think we are." Rafe tosses me the lighter and strides to the rented car.

"That's a depressing eye opener, man. Uh... thanks."

The taller man opens the car door and addresses me over the roof of the car. "It is what it is, Jon. Best you get used to the idea. I'll meet you back at the hotel."

I strike the lighter, the flame dancing in the fresh morning air of late spring. "Yeah. See you there." I let the flame die as the couple drives away.

As discussed, I'm going to light the blaze, make sure it takes where we need it and then put in a call to the firefighters. My cover story is going to be that I was driving alone on the isolated road when I saw the smoke. Staying here 'til I hear the sirens approach will ensure the fire doesn't spread to the woods before they arrive.

I head back to the front door of the mansion, regret washing through me at the loss of such a beautiful home. I flick the lighter on and off in my nervousness, twining through the house to light the spots Rafe indicated earlier.

A part of me desires to visit the room upstairs one last time... the room were Raine died. But I resist. The brutality of that moment is not how I want to recall the slim young wolf. I light the accelerants as instructed and hightail it out the back door. Fires don't run as rampant through a structure this large as one might think. All the doors on every floor are open to allow good air flow, but it still takes quite a while for the fire to reach the second floor.

Once it looks exactly as Rafe described, I call 9-1-1. "I'd like to report a fire."

I knock on the couple's hotel room door two hours later. I stopped off at my room first to eat, shower, and change clothes. I had to scrub three times to get the scent of the fire off of me. I debated on waiting until Rafe or Dria called me, but I have too many unanswered questions tumbling in my head.

Why did she refuse my blood when I offered? Why did Rafe want to talk to me privately when Dria was sleeping? Do the two speak with some kind of telepathy? That's got to be it, right? What else could those penetrating looks they exchange mean?

Rafe answers the door and stands aside, waving me in. He looks tired and drawn, but determined, too. "Did you eat or should I order food?"

"I'm good, thanks." I settle on the small couch and wait for Rafe to take a chair across from me. "Where's

Dria?"

He motions with his head toward a bedroom door. "She's still sleeping. Be out for a few more hours I bet."

I nod, unsure of how to approach him with the questions swirling around in my mind. Straightforward might work best. I clear my throat. "So... do you two speak in each other's minds?"

"Yes, we do. It's part of the mate bond we entered fifty-eight years ago."

I cough, choking on my own spit in astonishment. "Holy shit," I say when my voice clears. "Did you say fifty-eight years ago?" Rafe smiles and nods. "How freaking old are you, man?"

"I was past thirty when she finally agreed to bond with me."

"Damn, you look good for your age, you old fart."

"Ha-ha. Funny. Not."

"Oh, look at you, using modern phrases and everything."

Rafe shifts uncomfortably in his seat. "Laugh all you want, furball. A supernatural's ability to blend in will be what ultimately saves him or her from discovery."

"Look and sound like an ignorant sap and no one will notice you?"

"Something like that."

"Why did you want me to come here when she was sleeping? I got the impression you two share everything."

He looks toward the window, the bright sun creeps higher in the sky, approaching its zenith. "We do communicate frequently when we're awake, but we don't always have the same opinions on everything. We are still individuals no matter how tightly we're bound to each other."

"Are you telling me this so I'll understand what it's like when I bond with her and become her servant?"

"No," he rubs a hand over his face and lets out a deep sigh. "I'm telling you this because I know she plans to refuse your offer."

I sit up and lean toward him. "What do you mean by 'refuse my offer'? She already fulfilled her end of the bargain. I'm ready to live up to mine."

"She won't take you on as her servant because in the end, helping you was the right thing to do. Having you indebted to her for life to save the Weres doesn't sit right with her."

A cold settles in the pit of my stomach. Things were so much easier when I knew what I was getting myself into. I have a feeling this is the part he meant when they don't always share the same opinions. "But you feel differently, don't you?"

Rafe gets up and grabs a beer from the mini-bar. "Want one?"

I shrug. "What the hell. I don't have a job anymore. Might as well."

He tosses me a cold bottle and sits. "What was your impression of Dria today, when you saw her working on those Weres?"

"She was strong, determined, and tireless. She forged ahead with each person, never stopping to think of herself or the consequences of draining her strength too much. She proved to be a much better vampire than any of those pathetic creatures she killed."

"My wife is not just a better vampire, or simply a strong woman, she is desperately trying to hold onto her humanity with both hands, loving me with every ounce of her being to save the goodness within her, the goodness that was hidden deep for many years." He takes a long pull of his beer. "She needs me... and whether I like it or not, I think she needs you as well."

"Why me? Just for my werewolf blood?" A tiny part of me wants to ask why he doesn't like the idea of her needing me, but I wisely keep my mouth shut. Might humble me if my wife needed another guy, too, for any reason.

"Why do you think vampires crave an alpha's blood over another Were?" he asks.

"That's pretty obvious. We're more powerful."

"Yes, but it's much more than that. You *make* them more powerful, too."

Confusion wrinkles my brow. "I get that, that's why I offered to be her servant in the first place."

"Jon, that's not what I mean. You are strong enough to help her hold onto her humanity *with* me. She will be forced to look outside herself, and us, to see to *your* needs, being sure to never use or abuse you. Taking you on as her vampire servant will make her more compassionate and remind her of what it means to be human."

"Even though I'm not human anymore?"

"Yeah, furball, even then."

"So if she doesn't want me, what am I to do?"

A steely edge creeps into his eyes. "You plan to fulfill your pledge, right?"

I look around the room and gesture widely with my beer. "I'm here, aren't I?"

His face sets is a cold and unforgiving mask. "A man with honor follows his word willingly, not begrudgingly."

I look away from his penetrating stare. God, he's kind of creepy all on his own when he wants to be. "Alright," I say on a sigh. "You made your point."

"Be sure, Jon. There's no turning back. Do you want to serve a creature who walks the edge of darkness, clings to humanity by a thread, and will kill in the blink of an eye—or will you flee into the sun while she sleeps?"

Rafe's words give me pause. The only leader I had a lot of exposure to was Romeo. He did a fair job with the pack, but even he wouldn't put his neck on the line to save his own kind—something Dria did wholeheartedly once she agreed to help.

Out of everyone I've met in my time as a werewolf, she is the most honorable. A bloodsucking vampire. Who would have guessed?

I turn back and meet his bright blue eyes. "It would be my honor to serve her."

"Good." He stands and offers me his hand. We shake and a genuine smile creases his face. "I've got an idea on how to make this work. You'll need to buy a lot of chocolate for this to go off smoothly."

CHAPTER SEVENTEEN

"I'm sorry. What did you say?"

"Chocolate, man. You heard me. She loves it and can't eat it." Rafe ushers me toward the door. "You need to buy a pound or more and eat it all before you come back."

"Um... I really don't eat a lot of sweets."

"You need to eat it to tempt her into biting you."

Wait. I'm starting to get where he's going with this. "You want me to eat all the chocolate so she can't resist drinking my blood? Will that work?"

"That paired with the insatiable hunger she will be feeling when she wakes for the day should do the trick."

Fear grips me. "You mean I need to get her to bite me when she's starving? What if she loses control and drains me?"

"Hah! Not going to happen, Jon. She's going to fight her desires to drink from you the entire time, trust me."

"You won't be here to supervise?"

He shakes his head and opens the door. "Nope. I've

got to be out of here or she'll feed on me instead. Man up, Jon. You're going to have to play to her vampire hunger to entice her to bite you." He shoos me into the hall and props up the steel door with his body. "Combined with the blood she gave you earlier it will equate to a servant bond—assuming she drinks enough from you today. The lure of chocolate and the drain from altering the Were's minds should do the trick." He claps his hands together. "Hot damn. This may work after all."

He starts to close the door and panic grips me. What if I can't get this to work? "Wait!" He hesitates before it shuts all the way and opens it again, eyebrows raised in question. "Any kind of chocolate in particular?"

"Yeah. She likes dark best."

"Should I just come back here when I'm done?"

"And be quick about it. I'm not sure when she'll wake. I'll leave when you get here."

My stomach feels bloated with all the chocolate I consumed. I don't think any Halloween night or birthday party from my youth would rival what I voluntary shoved down my gullet this afternoon. Let's hope mixing Hershey's Special Dark with a couple of chasers of beer will do the trick.

I knock on the couple's hotel room door and glance nervously up and down the hall. Why do I feel like a cow being led to the slaughter house?

Maybe because you intend for her to eat you?

Panic grips me for a split second, but releases when Rafe swings open the door. He glances at his watch and gestures me in. "Good! Right on time. She should be waking soon. I can sense the change in her thought patterns. I was getting worried for a second that you might back out."

"I have to admit," I say with a forced smile. "Scarfing down that second pound of chocolate almost made me change my mind."

"No serotonin rush? That's supposed to be a 'feel good' hormone associated with eating chocolate."

I shake my head, raising a hand to press against my queasy middle. "With the first bar, maybe. After that, nope."

Rafe gives me a slip of paper with a phone number on it. "Here's my cell. I'll be in the gym for a while and then maybe hanging in the lobby. I don't think you'll need to call, but just in case."

I look around the empty living area. "Okay. What do I do until she gets up?"

Rafe shrugs, seemingly unconcerned. "You've got to be tired, right? Why not take a nap on the couch."

The idea of sleeping when the hungry vampire fifteen feet away could wake at any time unsettles me. I shudder, but don't voice my anxiety. "I'll watch TV. Don't worry about me."

"I'm not." He begins to leave and hesitates, turning back. "Listen, Jon. Dria was right that you could lose a bit of yourself in the bond. It's different for everyone."

"Did it happen to you?"

"No, but I'm not her servant. I'm her mate. We

won't know for sure how you're affected until it's done."

"And then what happens?"

"We deal with it." And with that parting comment, he leaves.

I return to the same couch I sat on a little while ago, debate on raiding the mini bar for liquid courage, but in the end I refrain and watch TV with the volume turned low. Somehow getting drunk when I'm trying to entice a vampire to bite me doesn't sound like a good idea.

There's a rerun of some pivotal football game from last season on cable and watching it requires little effort on my part. Gradually, my full stomach and the constant running from the past week catch up with me and my eyes drift lower. A peaceful relaxed feeling descends upon me, luring me to imagine the next couple of hours won't be so bad.

With a jolt I awake, Dria's intense green eyes staring at me from a few inches away. "What are you doing here, wolfman?"

I sit up, fumbling to turn off the TV in my haste. "I'm here to honor my end of the bargain."

"Isn't that interesting." Her fangs are fully descended when she speaks, but she doesn't lisp or stutter around the longer canines. "By my husband's absence, it's safe to guess he put you up to this?"

"We spoke earlier, yes. But it's the right thing to do. I made a promise and I intend to stand by it."

She waves off my words with a delicate gesture of one slim hand. "Pish-posh. You think I really care about that little deal we made?" She studies her perfect manicure. "You need to leave. Now."

"No."

Her gaze hardens, a glitter of her anger and restraint leaking in for me to witness. "Did you just tell me 'no'?"

I stretch out, putting my legs out in front of me, like I haven't a care in the world. Damn, this provoking a vampire shit makes me feel like I'm walking a tightrope over a river filled with crocs and piranha. Feigning nonchalance is harder than I thought. "Yup, I did. Guess your well-trained husband doesn't deny you much, huh Dria?"

In a split second she leaps and pins me to the back of the couch. Her mouth opens wide, salvia dripping off her sharp teeth to splatter upon my cheek. "Don't insult Rafe. He is no one's lap-dog. Least of all, mine."

"Hey, you're drooling there." I casually wipe my cheek. "Might want to watch that."

A short scream rips from her as she pushes away from me, shoving me into the cushion in her frustration. "Goddammit, Rafe! Where the hell are you?!"

She begins to pace back and forth across the room, her movements stiff and jerky.

"Come on, Dria. Just bite me and take what you need."

"Is that what this is all about?" She whirls around to face me, her hunger straining her every muscle. "I can resist you if I must. I've survived worse hunger than this before."

"I'm sure you have." I pat the couch next to me,

indicating she should take a seat near me. She ignores me and goes back to pacing. "But why resist when you don't have to? Why not let me take some of your burden and feed you from my strength?"

"You don't know what you're asking!"

I stand and approach her, still giving her a few feet safe distance. "Dria, look at me." Her gaze flicks briefly in my direction then jerks away. "I do know what I'm offering. I'm offering to pledge myself to you. To let you gain strength from me to use when you need it. To fight by your side no matter what the future holds."

"You make it sound so noble." She snorts. "Sounds like some shit Rafe filled you with." She continues to pace, her nervous energy driving her relentlessly. "It's not noble to lose your free will. It's not noble to put your needs before someone else's. It's not noble to want to give until you die!"

I reach out and grab her arm, hauling her around to face me. Her jaw snaps shut with a snarl. "It is when you trust the person you give your loyalty to."

She looks to the floor, her chest heaving. "You don't know me enough to give that kind of trust."

I give her a shake and force her attention on me. "You think so? Let me tell you what I do know—you have a husband who has stood by your side for well over fifty years. Would you say he gave his loyalty to you on a whim?"

"No, never. Rafe is different." Her eyes gaze off into the distance, past my shoulder. "He has experienced pain and suffering. He lived a life before he sought me out. He came to me knowing exactly what he was getting into. His eyes were wide open and his heart was pure."

"Well, I have no idea what life he led before marrying you, but I know my heart and mind on this." I reach over to the table where Rafe ate his meal and snag a steak knife. "And the choice is mine." I slice the serrated edge across my left wrist and watch the blood pool before running across my skin and dripping to the floor.

CHAPTER EIGHTEEN

The smell of fresh spilled blood fills the air between us. Dria's breathing becomes ragged as she stares at the red on my wrist. She shudders, but miraculously still resists.

"Dear God," she whispers. "Is that chocolate I smell?"

I wait to see if she'll act, but she doesn't, just continues to stare at the wound. "You're going to make every damn step difficult, aren't you?" Confused green eyes look up at me, like she's trying to process the sensory overload and make a responsible choice. I dip my fingers into the blood and reach toward her parted lips.

"No," she says, her voice a husky rasp of sound.

I ignore her and smear the sticky red across her full bottom lip. Her tongue darts out to taste my offer and another hard shudder wracks her frame.

"I don't like this. I'm usually the one doing the manipulating. I get the distinct feeling you two are trying to manipulate *me*."

"Oh come on, Dria. I want this. Your husband wants this. Why can't you give in?"

"Because I don't want to own you!" She tries to shake off my arm and this time it's me who holds her firm, forcing her to face what she doesn't want to see.

"Listen, vampire. You don't know me, but I think I'm strong enough to hold my own. I can't know for sure if I'll lose my free will, but I do trust you not to abuse me." Her faces closes down, no emotion on its surface. I have an inkling as to why she might be resisting so hard. "Have you had a werewolf servant in the past?"

She nods, the movement quick and jerky.

"I take it things didn't go well for him?" I ask.

"It was a 'her' and yes, things ended badly."

"Wouldn't it be safe to say you learned a lot from that bonding?" Her eyes search mine out again, uncertainty in their depths. "I bet whatever you think could have been done to change her fate has haunted you for years. Don't close yourself from another servant because of what happened. Learn from it and try again with me."

Silence stretches between us while the blood on my arm congeals.

"I do better with just Rafe in my life. I don't want anymore responsibilities."

"Let me carry some of your burden. Let me in. We can make this work."

Her body loses some of its tension. "Are you sure?" she asks.

As if I'm going to change my mind this late in the

game. "Yes, I'm sure."

Without another word she raises my wrist to her lips and feeds. With each pull from her mouth, my body floods with shockingly good feelings. It's like an endorphin rush from intense exercising combined with the allure of incredibly satisfying sex, the type where you hang limp and enjoy the afterglow as long as it lasts.

"Huh. I always wondered what the draw was to being bitten by one of you. Now I know."

She ignores me, completely engulfed in enjoying every drop she drains. In a moment the sexual surge dissipates to be replaced by the unmistakable feeling of pack. Warm furry bodies press against me in the woods, the odor of the fresh earth and scents of suitable prey to chase tickle my nose, and the hotel room fades into the background, along with the vampire sucking on my wrist.

No one distinguishing scent reminds me of any wolf I've met. All of them meld together to give me a feeling I've missed since the night I was attacked and changed into a werewolf—a feeling of home. The revelation shocks me to my very core. How can this slip of a vampire make me feel like I've finally found were I need to be? Could I be destined to mate with a woman who already has a husband? Would the fates be so cruel?

I try to block out the questions and relax into the experience. There's nothing sexual about her feeding, more that I can't shake the rightness I feel in this moment. Peace courses through me and I realize I'd follow this woman into the gates of Hell itself. And fight with every ounce of strength and cunning in me to bring us back alive.

After a few minutes she stops, licking my wound with a pointed tongue to stop the bleeding. A heavy sigh escapes her as she straightens. "Damn, Jon. That was really good. You tasted like dark chocolate. It was heavenly."

I smile, fighting the overwhelming urge to ask her to bite me a second time. I want to feel that way again. I want to feel it always. "Glad to oblige."

"You and Rafe were pretty damn sneaky. I bet he told you to eat chocolate, didn't he?"

"I plead the fifth."

"Hmph. Well Jon, you just bought yourself a ticket home with us. I can't promise things will always be smooth sailing between the three of us, but we can try our best and make sure we never lose respect for one another."

A thrill of excitement rushes through me at her simple words of acceptance. I did it. I got her to take my offer. "And where might home be?"

"Alaska."

~~*~~

Coming mid-April, 2015: A *V V Inn* "between the books" novella — free only to newsletter subscribers.

Three parts will be posted on www.cjellisson.com in

mid April, May, and June, then available for purchase at retailers in late June.

To sign up, copy and paste this site address into your browser's address bar: bit.ly/cj-news

A personal note from C.J.: If you enjoyed this book, please consider leaving a review on the product page where you purchased it. Reviews help readers discover new series and perhaps try an author they never heard of. Thank you!

About the Author: C.J. Ellisson lives in northern Virginia with her husband, two children, and three dogs. She's battled severe chronic illness for years and is thrilled to report she's finally approaching the end of treatment. She turned to writing when she could no longer work outside the home and claims the escape of penning contemporary erotic romance, urban fantasy, and erotica has helped save her sanity.

Death's Servant is the first prequel book in the *V V Inn* series and there are currently six novels and four prequel novellas planned, with more to be added if there is enough reader interest.

Books in the *V V Inn* series, in reading order :

Death's Servant, Prequel Story
Vampire Vacation, Book One
The Hunt, Book Two
Big Game, Book Three
Death Times Two, Book Four
Blood Legacy, Book Five

MORE places to connect with C.J.:

Website: cjellisson.com
Facebook: facebook.com/C.J.EllissonFanPage
Online Book Club: facebook.com/groups/
urbanfantasybc
Street Team: facebook.com/groups/cjeseethe

Do you miss signed books? C.J. offers free, signed promotional material from all her novels to readers who've left honest reviews on any retailer or book reviewing website. To obtain yours, please email your review URLs to admin@cjellisson.com with your mailing address—international readers welcome!

Acknowledgements

This book was written at reader request. I'm thrilled to finally be able to share one of the early *V V Inn* tales with all of you! Of course, in typical neurotic-writer fashion, I imagined all the juicy facts before I ever attempted to write the initial *V V Inn* books. It felt fantastic to discover my readers wanted to hear the creative histories I have swirling around in my head. As long as you all want to keep reading, I will do my best to keep writing these prequels.

I had about thirty dedicated alpha readers in my Facebook group for this story. Thank you for taking the time to share your thoughts and help me create a better story. If it didn't turn out the way you'd hoped, I'll take the full blame. ;-)

Big thank you to my most awesome editor, Tina Winograd. Your friendship and guidance in my work means a lot to me and I'm grateful to have you in my life.

As always, the biggest thanks goes to my husband, Pete. Your support during this last year as we struggle with medical bills and take out loans while we wait for royalties has been incredible. Thank you for every dinner, every load of wash, every trip the the store, and every reminder that I need to breathe and slow down. You're my reason for trying to succeed as a writer—so that some day I'll help support the family as much as you do.

Glossary of Terms and Characters

Bloodcoffee - a mixture of half-blood and half-coffee, favored by undead everywhere.

Donor - a human who donates blood to a vampire, willingly, with no connections.

Dria - the master vampire who narrates the first book, aka Vivian and Alexandria. She's married to Rafe and they own the V V Inn together.

Fledgling - term used for a vampire under the age of five years.

Jon/Jonathan - Vivian's werewolf servant and the head groundskeeper on the property.

Liebling - German endearment, meaning darling.

Master Vampire - a vampire who heads their own seethe, or is independent of a seethe. One not requiring the blood of a master to gain in power, but has accumulated enough strength to hold their own in a battle where an older vampire may try to drain a younger one for their blood.

Rafe - Vivian's human husband, bonded mate for sixty-five years, and co-owner to the inn.

Romeo - Jonathan's old Alpha, but not the Were who infected him.

Seethe - A vampire family, or group of vampires, with a master vampire at its head.

Turning - term used for when a human has been changed into a vampire.

Vivian - the nickname for Dria, a play on words from The V V Inn.

Were - shorthand for werewolf.